parrotfish

ellen wittlinger

SIMON & SCHUSTER BFYR

New York London Toronto Sydney New Delhi

for Toby Davis
with gratitude and admiration

SIMON & SCHUSTER BFYR
An imprint of Simon & Schuster Children's Publishing Division
1230 Avenue of the Americas, New York, New York 10020

Also available in a SIMON & SCHUSTER BFYR hardcover edition
Cover design by Lizzy Bromley
Interior design by Al Cetta
The text for this book is set in Baskerville.
Manufactured in the United States of America
This SIMON & SCHUSTER BFYR paperback edition October 2015
2 4 6 8 10 9 7 5 3
The Library of Congress has cataloged the hardcover edition as follows:
Wittlinger, Ellen.
Parrotfish / Ellen Wittlinger.
Summary: Grady, a transgender high school student, yearns for acceptance by his classmates and family as he struggles to adjust to his new identity as a male.
ISBN 978-1-4169-1622-2 (hc)
[1. Transsexuals—Fiction. 2. Identity—Fiction. 3. Family problems—Fiction.]
I. Title. II Title: Parrot fish.
PZ7.W7817 Par 2007
[Fic]—dc22
2006009689
ISBN 978-1-4814-6810-7 (pbk)
ISBN 978-1-4424-6681-4 (eBook)

Acknowledgments

Grateful thanks also to my editor, David Gale; his assistant, Alexandra Cooper; my agent, Ginger Knowlton; and Pat Lowery Collins, Anita Riggio, Nancy Werlin, and Kate Pritchard for their help and advice on the manuscript.

Special thanks to Toby Davis, without whom this book would not have been written.

Chapter One

I could hear Mom on the phone in the kitchen gleefully shrieking to her younger sister, my aunt Gail. I was in the garage, as always on the day after Thanksgiving, dragging out carton after carton of Christmas crap, helping Dad turn our house into a local tourist attraction and us, once again, into the laughingstock of Buxton, Massachusetts.

Dad handed me down another box from the highest shelf. "Sounds like Gail had the baby," he said. "You guys finally got a cousin."

"A little late for me to enjoy," I said.

"I'm sure she'll let you babysit sometime," Dad said, grinning. He knows how I feel about *that* job. But then his eyes met mine and his smile faded a little, as if he'd just remembered something important. No doubt he had.

I was separating forty strands of lights into two piles—white and multicolored—when Mom came flying through the screen door, her eyes all watery and glistening. "It's a boy!" she said. "A healthy baby boy!"

I dropped the lights I was holding and glared at her. Goddamn it, hadn't she learned anything from me?

"Healthy," Dad said quickly. "That's the main thing." *Thank you, Dad.* At least he was making an effort to understand.

"Of *course* it is," Mom said, trying clumsily to plaster over her mistake. "That's what I said. A *healthy* boy."

A chill ran down my back, and I turned away from them, imagining in my head the conversation between Mom and Aunt Gail. I do that sometimes to keep my mind off reality.

GAIL: Oh Judy, I'm finally holding my own baby in my arms!

MOM: So, tell me the important stuff! Is it a boy or a girl?

GAIL: A boy! A beautiful boy!

MOM: That's wonderful, Gail! A *real* boy!

GAIL: Do you have any advice for me, Judy? Since you always do everything perfectly, and I just struggle through life without a plan?

MOM: Glad you asked. You need to get yourself two more kids and a husband—so you'll be just like me! Of course, if you couldn't find a man before, having a squalling infant with a loaded diaper connected to your hip isn't going to help much.

GAIL: Oh, Judy, you know how much I hate you when you're right.

MOM: Well, don't worry—I'm hardly ever right in my own house anymore.

Okay, my mother isn't really that obnoxious to her sister. But when I imagine my little scenes in my head, I make people speak as if they weren't afraid of what other people thought. What they would say if they were suddenly turned inside out and everybody knew all their secrets anyway, so lying was beside the point.

But I *knew* the first question Mom asked Gail was, *Is it a boy or a girl?* Because, for some reason, that is the first thing everybody wants to know the minute you're born. *Should we label it with pink or blue? Wouldn't want anyone to mistake the gender of an infant!* Why is that so important? It's a baby! And why does it have to be a simple answer? One or the other? Not all of us fit so neatly into the category we get saddled with on Day One when the doctor glances down and makes a quick assessment of the available equipment. What's the big rush, anyway?

"She's naming him Michael. Michael Eli Katz. I'm so happy for her." Mom brushed away a stray tear, and I wondered who it was for.

Everybody would have been happy for Aunt Gail whether her baby was a boy or a girl. I knew that. *As long as it's healthy*—that's what they always say about babies. Why don't they say that when you're older? I was perfectly healthy, but nobody was applauding it anymore.

Dad got off the ladder and gave Mom a hug. "And now you're going to tell me you're off to the hospital this minute, aren't you?"

She smiled. "Sorry, Joe. I'm so anxious to see the baby. But I promise to help you set up the yard the rest of the weekend."

"Go on," he said. "The kids will help me."

"Actually, Laura wants to come with me," Mom said a little sheepishly, just as my younger sister slammed through the door, lips eggplant purple to match her thick eye shadow. Mom calls Laura's adventures with makeup "experimentation." I call them brainwashing by Maybelline.

"I've never been to a maternity ward before," Laura said, twitching her shoulders with excitement. "I want to see all the babies lined up in those little beds."

"Howling like Siamese cats," I said wistfully. Laura gave me an evil look.

"Charlie's staying here, though," Mom said, as if Charlie were ever any help to anybody.

"Don't worry, Dad," I said. "I'll help you."

"Angie, you should come with us," Laura said. "This is our first cousin."

"If you want to go, Angela, it's fine," Dad said. "We'll just work extra hard tomorrow."

"Nah," I said, "babies aren't my thing. I'd rather get Rudolph to balance on the roof ridge, and you know how much fun that is. Tell Aunt Gail I said congratulations. I'll be eager to see the kid once he can talk and tie his own shoes." Was it wrong to enjoy annoying my sister so much?

Laura smacked me on the shoulder. "Angie, you suck!" She generally found me exasperating, and I generally didn't care.

"Angela doesn't have to come along if she doesn't want to," Mom said, pointedly not looking at me. Disappointing her had become my full-time job.

"By the way, I've decided on my new name," I said. "So you can stop calling me Angela."

Laura huffed in disgust. "You aren't really doing that, are you?"

"I said I was. Didn't you believe me?"

"You can't just change your name overnight!"

"Sure I can. People do it all the time."

"So, what are we supposed to call you now?" Mom asked impatiently, the car keys jingling in her hand.

"Grady." I liked the way it sounded when I said it out loud. Yeah, it was good.

"'Grady'? What kind of a name is that?" Laura wanted to know. "Is that even a boy's name?"

"It's a name that could belong to either gender," I said. "Also, I like the gray part of it—you know, not black, not white. Somewhere in the middle."

"Grady," Mom said quietly, her eyes sweeping my newly short haircut.

"Nice name," Dad said as he climbed back up the ladder. He'd been amazingly calm about my recent declaration, but he didn't seem to want to discuss it much.

"It's a stupid name," Laura said. "What if we all decided to go and change our names? What if I decided I'd rather be called Cinderella or something?"

I shrugged. "Then I'd call you Cinderella."

"Or, what if I changed it to Madonna? Or, or . . . Corned Beef Sandwich!"

Mom gave her a push toward the driveway.

"Let's get going now. We can talk about this later."

"Bye now, Corned Beef!" I called. It looked to me as if Mom was having a hard time keeping a little smile off her face. I always could make her laugh.

I watched them slide into the car and pull away. No doubt they were complaining about me before they were out of the driveway.

LAURA: God, it was bad enough when Angie thought she was a lesbian. Now she wants us to call her by that dumb name. Why can't she just act like a girl?

MOM: [heavy sigh] Your sister never did act like a girl.

LAURA: And that horrible haircut she gave herself—ugh. It looks like somebody ran over her with a lawn mower. I'm so embarrassed when people find out she's my sister.

MOM: I always loved the name Angela. It was my first choice for a girl.

LAURA: [grumbling] You should have given it to me. It's better than Laura.

MOM: Another satisfied customer.

LAURA: You know, Mira's cousin is a lesbian, and she still wears makeup and dresses like a regular person. She's pretty, too!

MOM: [eyes glued to the road] Angela isn't a lesbian anymore, or so she says. She could still be pretty, though, if she'd wear decent clothing instead of those secondhand leftovers from the Goodwill.

LAURA: Are you kidding? Ma, Angie looks like Woody Allen dressed as a hobbit.

MOM: Oh, Laura, that's not fair. Angela is taller than Woody Allen.

I guess I don't really look like Woody Allen, especially since I got my contacts. But what do I look like? Kind of skinny. Kind of tall. Brown hair, shaved at the neck, floppy in the front. I look like everybody and nobody. Am I invisible? Probably not, because people sometimes stare. But I don't trust the mirror for this kind of information. Girl? Boy? The mirror can't even tell me that.

Why can't I act like a girl? I used to ask myself that question all the time. When the swimming teacher said, "Boys in this line; girls in the other," why did I want so badly to stand with those rowdy, pushy boys, even though my nonexistent six-year-old boobettes were already hidden behind shiny pink fabric, making it clear which line I was supposed to stand in? I wondered, even then, why I couldn't be a boy if I wanted to. I wasn't unhappy exactly; I was just puzzled. Why did everybody think I was a girl? And after that: Why was it such a big freaking deal *what* I looked like or acted like? I looked like *myself*. I acted like *myself*. But everybody wanted me to fit into a category, so I let them call me a tomboy, though I knew that only girls were tomboys, and I was not a girl. By high school I said I was a lesbian, because it seemed closer to the truth than giving everyone hope that someday I'd turn into a regular hairdo-and-high-heels female. I was just getting us all ready for the truth. I was crawling toward the truth on my hands and knees.

I came out once, but that was just a rehearsal—now it was time for the real thing. Because I was tired of lying. And the truth was, inside the body of this strange, never-quite-right girl hid the soul of a typical, average, ordinary boy.

Chapter Two

Dad and I dragged about fifty containers of junk out onto the front lawn, not to mention a dozen big standing figures. Fortunately it was a mild day, probably fifty degrees, so we didn't freeze our butts off like some years. It's always Dad and me who do most of the work anyway. Mom and Laura help, but they wear out fast, or they get cold, or they drop something on their toes, and that's the end of that.

"Should we do the hardest part first?" Dad asked. Which meant lashing a sleigh and nine enormous reindeer (counting Rudolph) onto the roof of the house.

"Can we do it with just the two of us?" I asked.

"Get Charlie to come outside. He can hold them in place while we run the guy wires."

Oh, there's an idea. "You want me to ask Charlie to *work*?" I asked. "He's playing Grand Theft Auto." As usual.

"I hope that's a video game and not a new hobby."

I nodded. "His favorite."

Dad sighed and looked away from me. "I don't know why we let that kid get away with loafing around all the time. He needs to start taking some responsibility around here."

Right, like someday Charlie would just decide *on his own* to stop being a spoiled brat. Dad acted like it was all a big puzzle, but he knew why the kid got away with murder as well as the rest of us did. Charlie was the baby, and apparently he would always be the baby, because he'd been born prematurely. Eleven years ago Mom and Dad had been scared to death that their tiny three-pound son would never make it out of the incubator. But he wasn't under the grow lights anymore—now he was a lazy, lumpy kid who spent his whole life parked in front of one kind of screen or another. Like me, he'd been born one particular way, and people thought that was who he'd always be, all evidence to the contrary.

So instead of positioning Donder and Vixen, we hoisted the fake chimney and one of the Santas—there were seven in all—onto the roof. They weren't as big as the reindeer, so it was only a two-man job.

Some of the packages that got piled into the sleigh had blown away last year, so I got out the shiny red-and-gold paper Dad likes and covered a bunch of empty boxes. Meanwhile, he set up the nativity scene down near the corner of the lot. You might think seven Santas *and* a nativity set *and* reindeer on the roof is holiday overkill. Ha! We were just getting started.

When the whole thing was set up—by Sunday evening, with any luck—there would be fake castle turrets clinging to the roof just above the gutters, outlined, as the rest of the house would be, by hundreds and hundreds of white lights. The roof scene would be in place: nine teetering reindeer statues (one with an electric nose) and a large sleigh piled high with "presents" next to the Santa with the perfectly arranged beard. Santas Two and Three (also plugged into the heavy-duty wiring system so they could wink every seven seconds) would be standing next to the pine trees on each side of the house, which would themselves be encased in strands of colored lights, tinfoil stars, and sixty-eight angel ornaments—unless we'd lost some since my last count.

Santas Four through Seven would be in place on the front lawn, attempting to play leapfrog with each other, although none of them actually move, so they would have to stay in their bent-over positions for an uncomfortable six weeks, after which we would pack them off to the chiropractor. To the left of the leapfrogging Santas would be Barbies on Ice, an addition Laura insisted upon when she was seven, which couldn't now be eliminated because the little-girl visitors loved it so much and huddled around it each year, worshipping Mattel. There used to be an even dozen Barbies in skates, but over the years a few were either stolen or eaten by wildlife, so we were down to eight identical long-legged sisters twirling in circles on a piece of magnetized plastic lit from below and controlled from inside the garage—Dad's finest electronic achievement. They were all dressed in white faux fur coats and hats, which took Mom and Laura an entire summer to sew. From a distance they looked like miniature dancing polar bears.

To the right of the lawn Santas would be the giant teddy bears having a picnic in the (fake) snow. Real snow had done a job on these guys, though—especially last year when we had three feet land on us in a two-day blizzard that buried them until early March. Their fur looked like old, matted shag rugs now and smelled like a cat box—probably because it was being used for that purpose.

I was hoping to get Dad to retire them, but I wasn't counting on it.

What am I forgetting? Plastic angels on the turrets . . . plastic poinsettias lining the sidewalk . . . plastic icicles on the windows. Oh, and the caroler statues near the front door who had speakers in their heads and were connected to the sound system in the living room so we could torture the neighbors with "The Little Drummer Boy" and "The Twelve Days of Christmas" every evening from six to ten. And not just for twelve days, either.

Dad and I were laying out all the wires that had to be hooked up, when I saw Eve coming down the street, obviously headed for our house. A good time for me to disappear into the garage and make sure all the cords were long enough to reach the main electrical box.

EVE: Hi, Angie. I'm lonesome. My snotty new friends aren't around today, so I thought I'd cut you a break. Let's just pretend like I haven't ruined our twelve-year friendship in my ridiculous quest for popularity, okay?

ME: Sure, Eve. Just throw me whatever scraps of your time are left over.

EVE: Great! I figured since I'm the only real friend

you have, you'd be willing to take what you could get.

ME: Yep, I'm begging!

EVE: But please don't tell anybody I was over here, okay? I wouldn't want my pretentious new friends to know I still talk to you.

ME: No problemo, Eve. If I see you at school, you're a stranger to me. Wouldn't want to jeopardize your social standing among the *important* kids.

Unfortunately, I couldn't stay in the garage making up my own scenarios for the rest of the afternoon, especially not after Dad called out, "Angela, Eve is here!" Obviously, it was going to take awhile to get my new name to stick.

I stood outside on the driveway but didn't go up to the two of them. I knew Eve would be making happy talk with Dad, giving him some lame excuse for why he hadn't seen her in weeks. I wasn't going to interrupt the performance. I pretended to be fiddling with one of the leaping Santas until she walked over to me.

"Hey, Angie," she said timidly.

"Hey."

"You guys putting your Christmas stuff out again?"

I just looked at her. Her twitchy little smile melted.

"You're mad at me, aren't you?" she asked.

"I don't see any reason to answer these obvious questions," I said. Eve could never stand to have anybody mad at her, even when she was really little. I'd taken advantage of it more than once over the years, making her apologize to me for stuff that wasn't really her fault. But this time she deserved my anger.

"Come on, Angie. Don't be mad at me. You're still my friend too!"

"Oh, *thank* you, Eve. I'm so relieved! Where am I on the list again? After Danya and Melanie and Zoe and—"

"That's not how it is!" She kicked her shoe into the nearest Santa, and it left a black mark. "Oops, sorry." She knelt down to try to wipe the mark off with a glove. "Why can't I have more than just one friend? I mean, they're my school friends and you're my home friend. What's wrong with that?"

"You mean I'm your runner-up friend. When Miss America, Miss Universe, and Miss Queen of the frigging World cannot fulfill their obligations. then I'm good enough to be seen with. Or rather, *not* seen with."

"Angie," she whined, "I need friends in my

own class. You remember how it was when you went to the high school for the first time and didn't know anybody. It's scary! I need more friends than just *one*!"

"Especially when that one is transgender, right?"

Eve opened her mouth to respond, but no words came out, so she shut it again.

"You kids want some cocoa or something?" Dad said as he passed us on the way into the house. "I'm gonna take a break and make myself some tea."

Eve's face came to life again for Dad—they've always been pals. "No thanks, Mr. McNair. I can't stay too long." As soon as Dad was inside the house, her smile disintegrated.

The reason Eve and I hardly knew anybody when we arrived at Buxton Central High School is that we were homeschooled from first grade through our freshman years by our mothers. Mom met Eve's mother, Susan, soon after their family moved into the neighborhood. They were both schoolteachers who had decided to stay home with their kids, and when they realized how close in age we all were, they decided to do a joint homeschooling thing, first with just us girls and then later with our younger brothers. My mom did the reading, social studies, and arts parts; Susan did the math and science. We all loved it, I have to admit. There were two "classes": Laura, Eve, and me in one and Daniel and Charlie in the other. Since we only lived a few houses apart, we'd walk back and forth when our "classes" changed. We all played soccer and took swimming lessons with kids from town, and when we listened to their stories about public school, it didn't sound like we were missing much. Crowded classrooms, too many worksheets, and lots of homework. We felt lucky.

I went off to Buxton last year, as a sophomore. The moms decided they weren't prepared to do higher math, and besides, I needed more "socialization." I think they hoped that being around boys would make me act like more of a girl. But it worked the opposite way. Seeing all that rampant girl-on-boy flirtation and boy-on-girl lust freaked the hell out of me. I couldn't figure out where I belonged in that picture. By the end of last year I came out as a lesbian, which, as I mentioned, was just a pit stop on the queer and confused highway. Over the last six months I started reading some books and going online to LGBT sites, and my feelings started making more sense to me.

I realized it wasn't just that I became

interested in girls when I hit puberty and started figuring out sex. I was a boy way before that, from the age of four or five, before I knew anything about sex. On one of the websites it said that gender identity—whether you feel like a boy or a girl—starts long before sexual identity—whether you're gay or straight. In my dreams at night, I was a boy, but every morning I woke to the big mistake again. Everyone thought I was a girl because that's the way my body looked, and it was crystal clear to me that I was expected to pretend to *be* a girl whether I liked it or not.

But you can only lie about who you are for so long without going crazy. So the week before Thanksgiving I cut my hair (not entirely successfully), bought some boys' clothes and shoes (easy), wrapped a large Ace bandage around my chest to flatten my fortunately-not-large breasts (much more painful than you might think), and began looking for a new name. I didn't expect it to be easy, but I figured that if I acted like this was a more or less normal transformation, maybe other people would too. The process was nerve-wracking, but it was a huge relief to know that my appearance was finally going to match my sense of who I really was.

Eve and Laura both arrived at Buxton High

this year, Eve as a sophomore and Laura as a freshman. (Laura didn't want to be the only one left in our "class," so the moms let her out early.) Laura had always had other girls her age from her dance classes that she hung around with, but Eve and I never needed anybody else—we'd been inseparable one-and-only friends since we were toddlers. When I came out as a lesbian last spring, it was the beginning of an uncomfortable distance between us that we tried to ignore. But it got worse when I announced the real truth.

Eve was looking at me sadly. "Oh, Angela!" She seemed to be begging for something, but I wasn't sure what.

"I'm not Angela anymore. My new name is Grady."

"Your new . . . what?"

"I told you I was going to find myself a new name. It's Grady. I'd like you to start calling me that. If you plan on speaking to me at all, that is."

"Angie . . ."

"Grady!"

"Whatever!" I could see tears in Eve's eyes, which is how I knew she was angry; anger and sorrow were always all mixed together for her. "Why are you doing this? So people notice you? I mean, everybody already thinks you're really weird!"

I took a deep breath and tried to stay calm. I knew I was going to have to figure out how to explain it to people. "You know, in Native American cultures people like me were honored. Before the Europeans arrived and screwed everything up, we were called Two-Spirit."

"Since when are you Native American?"

"I'm not, but—"

Eve shook her head. "I don't know what you want from me, Angie."

"Grady," I reminded her. "All I want is for you to use my new name."

She pressed her gloves into the corners of her eyes. "You act like that's a little thing! People are already talking about you since you cut your hair like that and started wearing men's shirts and stuff. Now I'm supposed to tell them that my friend Angela Katz-McNair isn't a *girl* anymore? That we should call her Grady and pretend she's a boy, or a *Two-Spirit*, or something halfway between one sex and another? They'll think I'm crazy too."

"Between two genders, not two sexes. I'm fairly sure my sexuality is just plain old heterosexual male."

Eve stared at me. "Angie, this is too confusing. I'm not like you. I need to have friends—I don't want people to think I'm a weirdo."

"You think I enjoy it?"

She thought about my question. "Maybe you do. At least you don't really *mind* it. If you did, you wouldn't put yourself out there like this. You're just asking for trouble."

"I'm just asking to be myself, that's all."

She shook her head. "Well, Angela was my friend, but I don't know who Grady is! I'm sorry, but I can't call you that in front of other people. I can't be part of this whole thing. It's too bizarre."

That fast I was back to being pissed off. "So I guess it's lucky you barely speak to me in school. My name change won't be a problem for you."

"I'm sorry, Angela. I hope we can still be friends—"

"When nobody is looking? Sorry, I don't call that *friends*." My voice careened into a shout. "And my name is Grady!"

Eve pulled her coat tightly around her body, as though she thought something inside might fall out. She scooted down the driveway and left me standing there, my biggest secret loose in the atmosphere between us. I'd been thinking of it as a clean rain, but obviously Eve thought it was air pollution.

I walked inside, shaking. Dad was sitting at the kitchen table, looking over the newspaper.

"I have kind of a headache," I said. "Do you mind if I stop for today? I'll help you again tomorrow."

"Angela—I mean . . ." He shook his head as if that would help the right name rise to his lips. "Gray . . . Grady, you're the only person in this house who enjoys helping me put up the decorations. You deserve some time off too." He winked at me and went back to the paper. I should have known that Dad would be the family member who had the least trouble with my change from daughter to son. Dad was addicted to happy endings. He'd do whatever he had to to finagle one, even if it meant drastically altering his idea of his own child.

On the way to my bedroom I passed Charlie grinning maniacally and shooting his way out of another felony.

Chapter Three

By busting our humps for two more days, we managed to get all of Dad's characters singing, skating, leaping, winking, and lying in a manger. Even Charlie was forced to abandon his joystick and remote control for a few hours in pursuit of our goal: the entertainment of greater Buxton by nightfall on Sunday. I didn't mind physical labor, and I'd always enjoyed working on projects with Dad—just not *this* project. If it had been a normal year, Eve would have helped out too. She always liked being there on Sunday when we put the finishing touches on everything. She'd stand back on the street and direct us as we moved statues a few feet this way or that. She had a good eye for details. But we got it done without her this year, and it looked fine.

I peeked from the garage door windows as the first visitors arrived, and though I couldn't hear their remarks, I could imagine.

LITTLE GIRL: Look at the Barbies! Oh, Mommy, why can't we do this at our house?

MOMMY: Because we have a life, honey.

GRANNY: [shaking her head] I wouldn't want to pay their electric bill.

LITTLE GIRL: I'd help you put up the decorations! Please, Daddy, can we?

DADDY: Right. Have you seen these idiots? They spent the entire four-day weekend doing this. I'd rather watch football.

LITTLE GIRL: [grumpy] I hate football.

MOMMY: [grumpy] I hate "The Little Drummer Boy."

GRANNY: Pugh! Those teddy bears stink!

Yes, our hard work and ingenuity were certainly appreciated, at least by five-year-olds. But the worst was yet to come. Now that the outside of the house was finished, we'd have to spend the next week getting the inside ready for display. As if mixing the Virgin Mary with the Virgin Barbies weren't bad enough, Dad liked to confuse centuries even further by turning the indoors into Queen Victoria's parlor. As far as Dad was concerned, if it had to do with Christmas, it was all good. You might think no one in their right mind would subject their family to this, but Dad's parents had done it to him, and he was passing the joy along to us. In fact, Dad probably became a carpenter just so he'd know exactly how to build his own house for maximum dramatic exposure.

Our living and dining rooms stretch across the front of the house, and each of them has a huge window that takes up most of the street-side wall. There are heavy curtains that pull across the windows, like you'd see on a theater stage. Which is what those rooms would become at night when the curtains were open. During the holidays we would put up a giant tree in each room and decorate it with paper chains, popcorn and cranberry garlands, and small oranges stuck with cloves. As a kid I liked making the paper chains, but now if they broke, I let Laura do the patching. The cranberries were easy, but stringing popcorn kernels onto thread is like trying to put a rope through a light bulb: Unless you're a magician, you end up with a lot of broken pieces in your lap. Nothing went on those trees that we hadn't made ourselves.

There were no electric lights used in the show rooms throughout the month of December, although candles, gas lamps, and two fireplaces gave off a golden glow. The fireplace in the living room had a platoon of toy soldiers marching through a miniature snow-covered village on top of the mantel. The dining-room hearth was swathed in holly branches and hung with five large stockings, made by Mom, with our names embroidered across their tops. (My old name, anyway. Maybe Mom would make one for Grady eventually.) Holly was also intertwined in the dozen wreaths that hung throughout the two rooms. Evergreen swags draped around the wall moldings, and sprigs of mistletoe hung from the ceiling. Both fireplaces were lit each evening at six o'clock and kept burning until we shut the curtains at ten o'clock. The rooms were supposed to look familiar to Charles Dickens should he happen to wander in off the street.

In order to keep things as authentic as possible, Dad didn't like us to go into these two rooms during viewing hours unless we were in costume. Nineteenth-century costume. So every year for the past ten years no one but Dad has used the two largest rooms in the house between Thanksgiving and January first. The rest of us would huddle in the kitchen or just stay in our own rooms upstairs, refusing to become character actors just to walk to our own front door. Dad, of course, was more than willing to get dressed up every night in order to light gas lamps and tend the fires. He put on heavy tweed pants and a woolen vest with a collarless white shirt underneath, the sleeves rolled up to his elbows, and wore one of those flat newsboy caps on his head. Nothing made him happier.

Obviously, Dad was a frustrated actor. Or maybe a thwarted set designer or something. He loved all this theatrical stuff, the idea that he was entertaining people. Except I think he was more entertained by it than anybody else.

The door slammed behind me. Laura and the usually immobile Charlie came up to the garage-door windows too.

"Who's out there?" Laura wanted to know.

"The Kellers. Mrs. Taylor and her kids. A bunch of people I don't know," I reported.

Laura grimaced and stamped her foot on the concrete. "Do we have to do this *forever*? It was fun when I was seven, but now it's just humiliating. You can't go out the door without the whole neighborhood staring at you. I'm so sick of having people walking around my house every night. Pretty soon they'll be looking in the windows again too. It's so stupid."

"Hey, you're the one who came up with the Barbies. That brings 'em back year after year," I said.

"I don't think it's so bad," Charlie said. "Except for those bears. And the music."

"You don't spend four days putting it all up, either," I reminded him. "Or taking it down."

"The music definitely sucks," he said, ignoring me.

"I bet everybody thinks we're just Santa's little elves or something, all happy and gay . . ." Laura glanced at me. "You know what I mean. Like Christmas is such a big deal for us. Like we're walking around singing 'Jingle Bells' all day. It's not true at all! We have an enormous nativity set in our front yard, and we never even go to church!"

"Not to mention that Mom is Jewish," I said.

"Exactly! I'm sick of opening my real presents in the kitchen so nobody sees that they're made out of plastic or spandex or something from this century! We have to get Dad to stop it," she said. "This has to be the last year."

"Fine with me," I said. "But who's going to tell him and break his heart?"

"I always forget Mom is Jewish. How come she likes doing this?" Charlie asked.

"Duh, Charlie," Laura said. "Mom hates all this—haven't you figured that out yet?"

"She doesn't act like it. She sews costumes and paints stuff. If she hates it so much—"

"I think she used to kind of like it at first," I said, "but now she just does it because she can't say no to Dad. Not about this, anyway. He *lives* for Christmas. He'd be miserable if he couldn't make our house look like the last stop for the Polar Express."

"And our living room look like Macy's front window," Laura grumped.

"Do you guys know those kids?" Charlie asked, pointing toward a group of teenagers clustered around the smelly bears, laughing.

"Oh my God!" Laura ducked down. "That's Sarah and Brit and their boyfriends! They're in my English class and I'm just getting to be friends with them. I can't let them see me!"

"Why? Don't they know you live here?" Charlie wanted to know.

Laura bent low and headed back inside. "I *hope* they don't! That's all I need—more news about my weird family for everybody to gossip about!" She glared at me, then sneaked back into the kitchen to hide. Poor Laura. Like Eve, she cared way too much about what other people thought.

SARAH: I would die if my parents put stuff like this out on our front lawn.

BRIT: You know who lives here, don't you?

SARAH: Who?

BRIT: Laura Katz-McNair. From our English class. The girl who wears the purple eye shadow.

SARAH: Really? Oh, no—I thought I liked her.
BRIT: Believe me, you don't. Her sister is that older girl who dresses like a boy.
SARAH: [sharp intake of breath] No! That he-she person? Oh, God—I feel so sorry for her!
BRIT: I know. Her whole family is obviously insane.
SARAH: That's so sad.
BRIT: It really is, isn't it?

"Mom told me you're changing your name," Charlie said matter-of-factly.

"Yeah. I want people to call me Grady from now on," I said.

He wrinkled his nose. "If I was going to pick a new name, it would be a cooler one than that." He started pounding on an old stool like it was a conga drum.

"Like what?" I asked.

He thought a minute. "Maybe Ryan. Or Keith. Or, no—Clive!"

"Clive?"

"It's better than *Grady*."

"Did Mom tell you why I'm changing my name?"

"Sort of. Something about how you want to be a boy now."

I nodded. At least Charlie wasn't having a hemorrhage over it like Laura.

"Actually, I think I always was a boy," I said. "I just didn't look too much like one."

Charlie glanced at me. "You do now."

"Well, I'm trying to now. But I always *felt* like a boy. So, now I'm going to start being one."

"Can you do that? Just decide to change?" He stopped drumming and stared up at me. "I mean, you don't have, you know, a penis or anything."

"No. But I don't think a penis is the only thing that makes you a boy. Do you?"

He seemed to be thinking it over. "I don't know. What else is different besides just body parts?"

"I don't think body parts are the whole story," I said. "I think the way you feel inside is more important."

"So inside you feel like a boy?"

I nodded. "More than a girl."

"Being a boy is cool," he said. "I'm glad I'm a boy."

"Well, I didn't decide to be a boy because it's cool. Being a girl is pretty cool too—it just didn't feel right to me."

He stuck a finger into his nose and fished

around a little. "I guess I get it," he said, but I had a feeling we'd be talking about it again when he got a little older.

"Does it bother you that I'm a boy?" I asked him.

He shrugged again. "It's kind of weird, but what do I care? You're not changing *me*."

"No, I'm not."

"You know, sometimes when me and Dan are playing Castle Killer, I like to be the girl character instead of one of the boys. The girl is the fastest one. I like to be fast in games because, you know, I'm not that fast in real life."

"But I don't just want to be different for a while. I want to be a boy forever. From now on. You get that, right?"

"Uh-huh." I don't know if Charlie was tired of our conversation or of standing on two feet, but he yawned and headed back inside.

It occurred to me that the male members of my family seemed to be taking this better than the females, and I wondered why that was. Did the women feel like I was deserting them by deciding to live as the other gender? Maybe for Dad and Charlie, it didn't seem strange to want to be male, since that's what they were. But Mom and Laura—and, of course, Eve—acted like I was betraying them somehow. Would I have to give them up if I wasn't a girl anymore? I hoped not. I hoped that changing my gender wouldn't mean losing my entire past.

Chapter Four

I came downstairs on Monday morning before Laura and Charlie. Mom was leaning against the sink, drinking her wake-up cup of coffee and looking out the window.

"Morning, Mom," I said.

"Good morning . . ." she said. An empty space hung in the air where "Angela" would normally have been inserted into the greeting, or where "Grady" might have been substituted. I had the feeling she'd been standing there preparing herself for my entrance but then couldn't quite make herself say out loud the name she'd been practicing.

I wasn't sure whether I'd been avoiding Mom all weekend or she'd been avoiding me, but we'd certainly managed to stay out of each other's way. I knew she was pretty freaked out by what had been going on with me lately, and I was wondering if things would ever be the same between us again. Not that we were that tight before—I always had more in common with Dad—but Mom had a good sense of humor, and sometimes we could get each other laughing hysterically about stuff. Would we ever be able to laugh and clown around like that—or even touch each other easily—the way we had before? Would she always have that sad look on her face when I walked into a room?

For the first time since I started understanding who I was, I wondered if the change was worth it.

"Is Laura almost ready?" Mom asked.

"Almost—still shellacking her face."

"Ange . . . honey . . . this new name . . . I don't know if I can get used to it."

I nodded. "Not ever?" My voice came out in a whisper.

She sighed. "I don't know. I feel like you're asking me to speak a foreign language. It's so strange. You're my *daughter*! I just can't think of you as my . . ." She poked a finger into the corner of her eye rather than say "son." The tear escaped anyway.

"I can wait," I said, "if it takes you awhile."

She made her mouth curve into a bad imitation of a smile and cleared her throat. "I wanted to tell you that if you want some nicer clothes—boys' clothes—I could buy you a few things. Some . . . shirts or something."

"I'm okay," I said. "I got some stuff at Goodwill."

"You don't need to wear secondhand clothes!" she yelled, her anger surprising us both. "Even if you're not . . . dressing as a female, you can still look well dressed. We can afford to buy you decent—" She put a hand up over her mouth as if she had to physically stop herself from saying more.

"I know that, Mom. I mean, I guess you can if you want to."

She took a deep breath and the sad smile popped up again. "You always had long arms for a . . ." She picked up my right arm and held it out. Why did her touch suddenly feel so rough to me? "Still, you're very thin. I imagine a men's small would be big enough for you."

"Are you sure? I mean, I don't want it to be tight."

Her gaze fell to my chest then, and for a moment I thought she was going to reach out and touch me there and feel the Ace bandage binding my breasts against my chest. Just thinking about it made the bandage feel tight and itchy, and I squirmed as she looked at me. I knew she was wondering how I'd gotten flat so suddenly; I turned away from her.

Even though my boobs weren't that big to begin with, this stupid bandage thing was *so* uncomfortable. I was definitely going to have to order the chest binder I'd seen recommended on a website. It looked like a close-fitting undershirt and was supposed to eliminate the shooting pains caused by this do-it-yourself method.

Laura came shuffling into the room, shoelaces dragging, and threw her book bag on the counter.

"Do we have any Pop-Tarts?" she asked, banging open cupboard doors.

Mom moved away then, and the tense connection between us fell away so quickly, it was as if gravity had been pulled out from under me. I felt like I might fall over or float off. As the two of them argued the merits of Pop-Tarts versus cereal, I tried to calm down and pretend it was just an ordinary day.

But I knew it wasn't. It was the day I was going to school with my hair parted and combed the way a boy would, my chest bound tight under a boys' flannel shirt that was tucked into a pair of boys' baggy jeans. It was the day I was going to the principal's office to ask that my name be changed on all my records. It was the day I planned to ask my teachers and classmates to call me by my new, neutral name, Grady. It wouldn't be an ordinary day. It would be the day that, for better or for worse, I became myself.

Laura leaped out of Mom's car before it had even come to a full stop in front of the school.

"Laura!" Mom called after her. "Are you staying after school for anything?"

"Maybe!" Laura yelled. "I'll call you!" She was already halfway up the front steps.

I took my time getting my backpack together and climbing out so Laura could make a clean getaway.

"You need to be picked up today?" Mom asked.

I shrugged. "If you're not coming for Laura, I'll just walk. Weather's good."

She looked uncertain, even a little afraid. "Well, you can always call me if you want to. I'll be home."

"Okay." I guess she thought Grady would need her protection more than Angela had.

A few kids stared at me as I walked inside the building, but nobody said anything. I figured they'd gotten used to me looking different little by little as I went from tomboy to lesbian to short-haired guy-in-a-flannel-shirt. As I headed for my locker, I could hear Eve's laugh—not her real laugh, but the high-pitched, phony-sounding laugh she'd begun using since her arrival at the high school. I turned around to see her standing with her new pals outside the door to their first-period French class. Her eye caught mine for just a second, but she immediately turned her back to me. Before this year I never would have believed I'd see that: Eve ignoring me. For a dozen years she'd been my shadow, my henchman, my one and only friend—and now she wouldn't even look at me. How could she do this to me? Of course, she thought I was the one who'd done something awful to her.

I watched her twirling her wavy, slow-to-grow-out hair around her index finger—her *I am nervous* signal since she was five. Her pasted-on smile flitted from Danya to Melanie to Zoe, begging them to grin back. No such luck.

"Will you stop doing that thing with your hair, please?" Danya said, pushing Eve's hand away from her curls. "You're driving me crazy." She reached back to tighten her own long ponytail—straight, blond, perfect.

"Sorry," Eve said, cringing like a puppy who'd just been caught peeing on the carpet. Why did Eve want to hang out with such obnoxious people? I had to look away.

"Hey, Angela."

I wheeled around. "Oh hi, Sebastian." Sebastian Shipley, a guy I knew from TV Production class and Cable Club, had his locker near mine. He was short, skinny, and quite the nerd, but always friendly. One of those kids who live on such a distant planet, they don't understand the laws of high school, or even know that there *are* laws. He spoke to everybody all the time, and everybody from the jocks and the popular kids to the Goths and the hip-hop wannabes were so stunned by his lack of awe that they actually spoke back.

"What video are you doing next?" he asked.

"I'm not sure what I'm shooting—I have to check the schedule. I'm editing the final boys' soccer game right now. It airs Thursday."

Buxton's local-access cable TV studio was located at the high school, and any student who took TV Production could join the Cable Club and help program the channel. It was the best thing about going to Buxton High, in my opinion. I'd already learned how to shoot and direct a show, and now I was learning digital editing too.

Sebastian nodded. "I have to finish editing an elementary-school Thanksgiving program this week. I hope I don't get assigned to film a bunch of little kids' Christmas programs—they're so boring. I'm going to ask Mr. Reed if he'll schedule me to shoot the Winter Carnival dance."

"Really?" I was surprised. Sebastian Shipley didn't seem like the type of person who'd want to go to a big, fancy dance. He was friendly, sure, but I was pretty certain he'd never had a date or gone to any of the usual school functions. He was a guy who was always alone and seemed okay about it.

"Sure. I wouldn't go otherwise, and I like seeing everybody all dressed up like that. The girls look so great."

Sebastian noticed girls? Huh. I guess everybody has hormones.

"Are you going?" Sebastian asked.

"Where? To the dance?"

He nodded.

"No way." I laughed. "Not my kind of thing."

He smiled. "Me either. You know, if I don't get to film it, I mean . . . maybe we could go to it together?"

This day was turning out even weirder than I thought it would. "What?" I gasped. "You want me to—"

"I know I'm a lot shorter than you are, but that doesn't bother me," Sebastian said. "It wouldn't be like a real date or anything. It would just be fun to dress up and go. Don't you think? I've never gone to a dance before."

No, I absolutely did *not* think. Obviously, Sebastian would have to be told the whole story, now. "Look, Sebastian, there's something you should know. I'm changing my name. I'm changing my whole life—"

"Cool! What's your new name?"

"It's Grady, and—"

"Grady. I like it. I liked Angela too, but—"

"Look, Sebastian, Grady is a . . . a boy. I'm a boy now."

The first bell rang as Sebastian looked up into my face.

"So I can't really go to the dance with you. Because, you know, we're both guys. And I'm not gay or anything."

I grabbed my English books from the shelf, shoved my backpack into the locker, and slammed it.

Sebastian was staring at me by then, his mouth open wide, his eyes sparkling with amazement, as though I'd just announced my virgin birth. "Wow!" he finally managed to say. "You're just like the stoplight parrotfish!"

What? "Uh-huh. Well, I have to motor, Sebastian. I've got English—" I started to back away from him.

"I'm doing a report on them for Environmental Science! The stoplight parrotfish!" He was practically yelling now, and people were turning around in the hall to look at him.

"Yeah, okay—" *Whatever.*

"I'll tell you all about them when we get to TV Production!" he said. "You won't believe it!"

I ran for the stairs. *That* was a reaction I wasn't expecting. God, the kid was more interested in some fish he was doing a report on than the fact that the girl he asked to a dance told him she was really a boy. Was the rest of the day going to be this strange?

Mrs. Norman, my English teacher, was erasing the board when I walked in, so I took the opportunity to sidle up to her, trying not to make a big production out of it.

"Mrs. Norman?"

"Angela." Mrs. Norman never used a spare word if she didn't have to.

"I'd like to ask you a favor. Um, I'm changing my name."

Mrs. Norman continued to erase, keeping her back as stiff as a tree trunk. I hadn't yet penetrated her force field.

"I'd like you to call me Grady from now on instead of Angela. That's my new name. Grady."

Finally she put down the eraser and looked at me. "Have you talked to Dr. Ridgeway about this?"

"Not yet. I plan to go there before lunch and ask him to change my name on my permanent records."

The second bell rang, and Mrs. Norman started writing some ten-syllable words on the board. "I'm sure Dr. Ridgeway will notify all your teachers if and when he approves the change," she said.

What? "Well, the thing is, Mrs. Norman, I'm changing my name whether Dr. Ridgeway approves of it or not. And I'd like to be called Grady. So I'd appreciate it if you'd call me that now."

Finally she looked at me. "Angela, it seems to me that changing one's name is nothing more than an attention-getting device. I see no reason to disrupt my classroom just because you've made a rash, momentary decision. You may decide by tomorrow that you want to change your name back again!"

"I won't, though. I'm never going to be Angela again."

But she was through with me. "Take your seat, please. Second bell has rung."

I sat down. I hadn't even told her *why* I wanted to change my name. I could imagine that conversation.

ME: I'm a boy now, Mrs. Norman. Grady. A guy, not a girl.

MRS. NORMAN: Don't be ridiculous, Angela.

ME: No, really, I'm a boy.

MRS. NORMAN: Why do you feel the need to call attention to yourself like this, Angela?

ME: Believe me, if I only wanted attention, I'd find an easier way to get it.

MRS. NORMAN: Is this some silly idea you came up with over the Thanksgiving weekend?

ME: Actually, I've been thinking about this for months. Years, even.

MRS. NORMAN: I suggest you take a yoga class, Angela. Rather than become a . . . [shivers] male. Learn to breathe deeply and stand up straight. Good posture is the key to mental health.

ME: I'm not mentally unhealthy, Mrs. Norman. I'm just a boy.

MRS. NORMAN: Really, Angela, get hold of yourself. By tomorrow you'll want to be a girl again. Girl, boy, girl, boy. You'll have everyone confused.

ME: No, I won't. And I won't be confused anymore either.

MRS. NORMAN: Take your seat, Angela, or I'll hit you with an eraser.

Mrs. Norman called on me three times that hour, singing out all three syllables of "Angela!" as loud as possible. Bitch.

Ms. Marino, my Spanish teacher, was easy. It was her first year teaching, and she just wanted us all to like her. I could have said, "Please call me Wolfgang Amadeus Mozart from now on." I could have told her I'd decided to become an elephant or a lilac bush and she'd have said the same thing.

"Why, that's wonderful! I'm so happy for you, Grady! *¡Mis mejores deseos para tí!*" Then *she* called on me three times, always shouting out "Grady!" at the top of her lungs, rolling the *R* so it sounded vaguely Spanish. Apparently, Mrs. Norman was right: Changing my name was getting me way too much attention, especially from teachers.

The half-awake kids in my Spanish class didn't seem to care what name I was called. I barely ever spoke to any of them anyway, except when forced to converse in our foreign language.

"Para la merienda, ¿quieres la chuleta de puerco o la sopa?"

"Mi comida favorita son las chuletas de puerco con arroz."

As if the high school cafeteria ever served a recognizable pork chop anyway.

Next class, however, was gym. I'd been dreading

it the entire Thanksgiving vacation. Gym was one place it mattered very much whether you were a boy or a girl. There was no gray area for Grady—you either changed clothes in the boys' locker room or the girls'. And I could no longer imagine using either one. Unbinding my boobs to step into the girls' shower? I didn't think so. The *boys'*? Right. Or I could just jump into an active volcano.

Ms. Unger and Coach Speranza cotaught gym class. Sometimes the boys and girls did stuff together, and sometimes we split up according to gender. I wasn't crazy about Ms. Unger, but I'd never be able to put up with Coach Speranza for the rest of the year. He was the kind of gym teacher who encouraged the athletes to make fun of the kids who had a hard time huffing around the track or getting to the top of the climbing rope. He believed public humiliation was a teaching tool. Even Ms. Unger didn't like him, and she wasn't such a sweetheart herself.

I found Ms. Unger in her office just inside the door to the girls' locker room, bent over a newspaper that was spread open on the floor. She looked up at me from her task of digging dog shit out of the crevices of her sneakers.

"Right in the middle of the track!" she said, as if I'd asked her a question. "There's a sign out there begging those idiots to pick up after their mutts, but they ignore it. Somebody could slip in this and break a leg. One of these days I'm gonna catch one of those morons, and *then* they'll be sorry!"

Ms. Unger's tirades always scared me a little bit. She got so mad over the dumbest stuff. I just stood there watching her work.

"Did you want something? You're not gonna ask to be excused from gym today, are you, cowboy?" It was obvious that I'd be sorry if I did. When Ms. Unger started calling people cowboy, it usually meant her patience had been stretched thin.

"No," I said. "But I wanted to talk to you a minute."

"So talk," she said, digging at the sole of her shoe.

"The thing is, I'm changing my name. I'm going to the principal's office next period to tell him about it too. I'd like people to start calling me Grady." I smiled, hoping to appear likeable and harmless.

Ms. Unger put down the shoe and looked up at me. She squinted her eyes. "Don't tell me."

Her gaze took in the haircut, the shirt, the pants.

"Good Lord," she said. "You're transgender, aren't you?"

My mouth fell open. "Well, yeah. How did you know?"

"I'm not blind," she said. "And I'm not a math teacher—I'm a gym teacher. And you're not the first one."

"I'm not?"

She sighed. "About five, six years ago. It was a boy, though, going the other way. Mr. Gleason was teaching with me then—not *Speranza*." She said the name as if it were something else she'd scrape off the bottom of her shoe. "We handled it together. Couldn't use the girls' locker room, but we certainly couldn't make the kid use the boys'. She'd have been cream cheese in five minutes."

I flinched at the image.

"So you want to know what room to use, don't you?"

I nodded. "And when we split up, do I stay with you or . . ."

"My advice? Keep away from Coach. He'd love to scramble your eggs. Do you feel comfortable staying with the girls?"

"Sure. I mean, I grew up with girls. Even though I know I'm a boy, I don't exactly know how to *be* a boy." I was surprised at what a relief it was to be able to talk to somebody who knew about this, who wasn't terribly shocked by the whole idea.

She nodded. "Okay. Well, here's what we'll do. I've got a bathroom and a shower in here, in my office. You can use them during gym class or whenever you need to during the day. I'm not in here that much anyway, unless I've stepped in dog crap. At least for now, stay with the girls. We'll hope nobody raises a stink about it."

"Do you think they will?"

"No way to know. Sometimes people are great. Sometimes they're jerks. If you have any problems, come talk to me, okay?"

"Okay." *Who'd have thought Ms. Unger would be so cool?*

"What did you say your new name was?"

"Grady."

"Grady, before you put your gym clothes on, how about helping me out here?" She handed me a sneaker and a knife.

We bent over the newspaper together and dug poop out of the soles of her shoes, which was the high point of my day so far.

Chapter Five

I'd been so worried about gym class, and then it turned out fine. Nobody seemed to notice that I'd changed clothes in Ms. Unger's office. They probably would eventually, but for today it was easy. Of course, I didn't make a big announcement about it or anything. Ms. Unger called me Grady once, and a few girls turned around to see who she was talking to, but most of them just looked right through me like they always did. We ran the track—inside—and then played volleyball as usual. Well, not quite as usual. Wearing that damn bandage made it hard to get a deep breath, and my ribs were aching by the time we finished. I wondered how long it would take for the undershirt binder to arrive if I ordered it that night.

I was so relieved about gym class that I felt optimistic walking into Dr. Ridgeway's office. So what if kids called him Dr. Rigid Way or Dr. No Way? He'd always been perfectly nice to me before. His secretary smiled and told me I was in luck—he had a few minutes free. And I *felt* lucky as I walked in and closed the door; everything was going pretty well.

"So, Angela, sit down, dear. What's going on? No problems, I hope?" Typical Dr. Ridgeway. He hated for there to be problems. He called himself a problem solver, but really he was a problem avoider.

"Well, not exactly a problem, Dr. Ridgeway."

That made him happy—he grinned.

I plunged in. "But there is something I need to talk to you about. I'm changing my name. I intend to start living as a boy."

His smile twitched and wriggled and finally fell apart. "Oh, Angela, my dear. No, no. You don't want to do that."

"Yes, I do, Dr. Ridgeway. I've already spoken to my parents about it and they're going to call me Grady." Okay, something of an exaggeration. "And I want everyone at school to call me that too."

He shook his head. "You don't understand what you're letting yourself in for, Angela. There's no need to go overboard. We're a liberal community—dress boyishly if you like—but to change your name and announce it to everyone? What's the point of that? Terrible idea." He slammed shut the dictionary that was sitting on the desk in front of him, as though he'd just given the last word on the subject.

I leaned back in my chair, stunned by the look of aggravation on Dr. Ridgeway's face. Dr. No Way. What did he think was going to happen to me that was worse than lying all the time? I couldn't go back to being a girl; even if somebody beat me up for doing this, I couldn't.

"I don't really think I have a choice, sir," I said. "I *am* a boy. I can't pretend anymore that I'm not. And I don't want to."

Dr. Ridgeway leaned across his desk and glared at me, almost as if he were angry. "Well, Angela, that's just silly. Of course you aren't really a boy. You're probably a lesbian—I understand that. And I suppose you want to prove something by going all the way like this. Pushing the envelope, they call it. But I'm telling you, for your own good, I can't condone it. I'm sorry."

"I'm *not* a lesbian. And this *is* for my own good, Dr. Ridgeway. Don't you think I know what my own good is?"

He gave me a sad and knowing smile, the kind adults give you that makes you seriously consider homicide. "No, I don't. Teenagers rarely know what's good for them, I'm sorry to say. Take my advice now, Angela, and don't tell anyone else about this. In a few years you'll be in college, and then you can act as outrageously as you want to and no one will care. Although by then you'll probably have forgotten all about this silliness. But for now, be careful. I don't want to see you get hurt. And I don't want to see my school get turned upside down for nothing, either."

Right. That was obviously the bottom line: Don't rock the boat. Don't start trouble that he'll have to deal with. I should have known.

"So you won't change my name on my records?"

"No, I won't. If your parents come in and ask me to change it, I might reconsider. But I doubt that they're too pleased with this idea either."

I stood up. "You can't stop me from telling people," I said.

He looked like he wished teachers could still whack kids on the knuckles with rulers. "No, I can't. But I'm warning you, no good will come of it."

I felt so miserable walking out of there. Why had I expected Dr. Ridgeway to understand? Did I really think that he'd say, *Of course, Grady! Let me just make a note of that new name. Good choice, by the way!* What world did I think I was living in?

Would Mom or Dad come to the school and argue for my right to choose my own name, my own gender? Mom was having trouble using

"Grady" herself; maybe she'd agree with Dr. No Way that the new name would only cause trouble. And Dad hated talking to any kind of school administrator. He had some leftover anxiety about authority figures from back when he was in school. He didn't even like talking to teachers, which was funny because he'd married one. No, it wasn't too likely that I'd get them to stand up for me.

As I walked down the hall, three lunkhead bozos who thought they were hilarious came around the corner and "accidentally" crashed into me.

"Oh look, it's Angela Cat-Hair!" the first idiot said.

"Oh, wow, I thought for a minute it was Angelina Jolie! There's such a resemblance."

"Hey, Cat-Hair got a haircut!" One of them started messing up my hair, and I knocked his hand away.

"Ooh, Hairball is in a fightin' mood," the fool said, making hissing sounds and clawing the air with his fingernails.

When they assumed martial-arts positions, I walked away. They fell all over themselves with hilarity.

"Bye now, Cat-Hair!"

"Have a nice day, Hairball!"

Ha, ha. I could hardly wait for my latest news to filter down to moron level. They'd enjoy it immensely.

Suddenly I was feeling like a big old piece of that stuff I'd scraped off Ms. Unger's shoe. I slunk into the cafeteria, hungry but feeling a little sick to my stomach, too. I was standing in line, waiting to get the daily slop, when I noticed the group of girls across the room looking at me and pointing. Well, Danya was pointing. Melanie and Zoe were just staring out from beneath their thick waterfalls of hair. Eve was busy examining the noodles in her soup.

Head high, Danya strode across the room and stopped a few feet away from me. "Is it true?" she asked in a loud, shrill voice that could make dogs whimper. Talk about somebody looking for attention.

"Is what true?" I said.

"We heard you're not a girl anymore. You changed into a boy named Grady."

The line inched forward. "You got the gist of it," I said.

She wrinkled up her nose as if I suddenly smelled bad. "That is so sick! I've never heard of anything like that! It's disgusting!"

People were looking at us now and whispering.

I tried to act calm, even though I felt shaky inside. "I thought you *liked* boys, Danya. I thought you were a big fan of the male species."

"Real boys, yeah. Not freaks who *think* they're boys."

Eve had come up behind Danya. She put a hand on her buddy's arm. "Danya, you wanted to see my history notes, didn't you?"

Danya swung around and pulled her arm away from Eve. "I'm talking to your *boyfriend* here, Eve. How could you ever have been friends with this mutant? Didn't you know she was weird?"

Eve blushed. "I . . . Angela wasn't . . . I mean, when she was a she—"

"She's still a she! You can't just decide you want to be the other sex!" Danya said.

Eve was careful not to make eye contact with me. "I know. I'm just saying, Angela never told me—"

"You better not have a crush on this he-she person, Eve. If I find out you've been hanging around with this pervert—"

"Danya, let's *go*!" Eve said, then ran back to their lunch table. Zoe and Melanie followed her, but Danya stood there staring at me another long minute.

"I better not ever hear that you tried to get

together with Eve, you freak. My father is a policeman, you know."

By that time my hands were shaking too. "And what's he going to do? Arrest me for cutting my hair? Or changing my name? For being different?"

She sneered. "*Different?* You make the different kids look normal!" Then, with everybody in the room quiet and looking at us, she turned and stalked out the door.

There was no way I was eating lunch after that. There was no way I was hanging around the cafeteria, either, now that I'd become the hot topic for lunch gossip. And then, as I hurried down the hall toward my locker, I felt a twinge of pain low down in my abdomen, because apparently a bad day can always get worse. Already kids were whispering about me as I passed them, maybe using the same words Danya had. *Freak. Mutant. Pervert.* And now I was a boy who had just started his period and was probably bleeding all over his jockey shorts. Yeah, that was normal.

Even my own body betrayed me on a regular basis. What was I supposed to do now? Crap. I could feel the cramps advancing. The gym and Ms. Unger's bathroom were half a mile away from my locker. By the time I ran down there I'd be a mess. And who knew if she'd have any pads in there for me to use anyway?

I grabbed my pack from my locker and looked up and down the hall, weighing my options. There were restrooms not far away, but which one could I possibly go into? If I went into the girls' room there might be some crazy creep like Danya in there who'd ream me out just for existing. On the other hand, if I went into the boys' bathroom, who knew what might happen? No doubt some of those hormone cases would be thrilled to bloody a nose. They'd put it on their resumes for Bigot College.

No, there was enough bleeding going on already, and no place to hide, even for a few minutes. I thought of Dr. Ridgeway. *No good can come of it.*

The pay phone was in the lobby by the exit. Better to huddle here and wait instead of walking the halls and displaying any possible seepage. "Mom," I said after she answered, "I'm not feeling well. Can you come and get me?"

Chapter Six

As soon as I got in the car, I closed my eyes and leaned back against the headrest, but I could tell Mom was staring at me. After a minute she said, "So, what happened?"

"Nothing happened. I got sick. I told you."

"You weren't sick this morning."

"Sickness doesn't have a special time of day, you know. It just starts." I knew she knew I wasn't really sick, but I didn't feel like going into any details. Admitting I had cramps seemed like an argument against what I'd been trying to prove to her. And I certainly wasn't going to tell her about my talk with Dr. Ridgeway or the run-in with Danya. I could just hear her saying, *I knew this would happen.* Mothers always know something rotten is going to happen to you, because they're always worried about every little thing anyway. So the one out of twenty times something bad does happen, they're sure their psychic mother-knowledge foretold it.

She didn't say anything else until we pulled into the driveway. Then she announced, "Gail is here with the baby. Let's not upset her."

"I wasn't planning to," I said, climbing out of the car and slamming the door harder than I intended. Jeez, Mom was the one who usually got Aunt Gail upset, not me.

The new mother was propped in the corner of the living-room couch with pillows stuffed under her arms so the baby would be at the right height to breastfeed. It seemed strange to see Gail like that—so quiet and intent, staring down at that small, bald head as if the secrets of the universe were written there. Not to mention the fact that my skinny, athletic aunt had her shirt pulled up over her newly ginormous boobs, which were currently being used as a snack bar.

I waved to her and said, "One second," then hurried upstairs for some damage control before my first meeting with the babe.

"Hey, cousin!" I whispered, sitting down gently next to the twosome. Talking in my regular voice seemed too intrusive. The baby was curled into Gail's chest like a large kidney bean, motionless except for his sucking cheeks.

"Hi, honey. Meet my little miracle." Gail looked up at me and smiled, then suddenly startled. "Are you sick, Angie? You shouldn't get too near . . ." She started to pull the baby away from me, and he flung out his arms like a contestant on *American Idol* appealing to the crowd.

"Don't worry," Mom said. "She's not really sick."

Gail relaxed, and the baby glommed back on to her breast. "Just taking some mental-health time?" she asked.

"Something like that," I said.

"You got your hair cut," she said.

"She cut it herself," Mom said. "Can't you tell?"

"Why'd you do that? I would have cut it for you. Don't I usually cut it the way you like it?" Gail looked a little hurt.

"Sure—it's just that I wanted to try something a little different for a change."

"It makes you look like a boy," she said.

Mom and I looked at each other; obviously this was the way in which I wasn't supposed to upset Aunt Gail. But the silence got longer and weirder until finally Mom was the one who said, "That's the point."

But Gail wasn't really paying attention. She was staring into Michael Eli Katz's eyes. "Isn't he beautiful?" she said. "I know all mothers think their babies are beautiful, but Michael really *is*, isn't he?"

We assured her he was, although I have to admit that all babies looked pretty much the same to me: puffy little bodies with squashed-up faces. She lifted him up onto her shoulder and rubbed his back until he burped and dribbled milk down her shirt. Mom got a towel to clean things up, but I was pretty sure Gail wouldn't have cared if Michael had puked all over her. He was her little miracle. At least for now. I wondered if she'd still adore him so much once he got a personality of his own.

When the baby fell asleep, Gail put him down in the little basket she'd brought along, and she straightened her disheveled clothing. Mom brought us all tea at the dining-room table.

"So," Mom said as she put a large cup in front of her sister, "do you still think you'll be able to go back to work in three months?"

Gail's spine stiffened. "I don't have a choice about that, Judy. I wish you'd stop acting as if I did."

"I'm just saying, now that you know what it's like to have a baby . . . you see what I mean, don't you, about how hard it is to leave them with strangers?"

"Of course it'll be hard to leave him! I know that! But Jackie is hardly a stranger. I've known her since high school, and she's been running her day care for ten years—"

"I just feel sorry for him, that's all. To have to

go to day care at such a young age." Mom looked sadly over at Michael's basket as if she were watching bad luck rain down on him. She must have known the effect this would have on Gail.

"Why do you keep bringing this up? I'm raising this child by myself, Judy. I don't have a husband—I have a sperm donor! There's *no choice*. If I want to be able to feed and clothe my son, I have to work. Full-time. I knew this when I got pregnant, and so did you. It was either be a single working mother or not be a mother at all. I can't make the choices you made, but that doesn't mean I won't be the best mother I can be!" The tears were running in little rivers down her face. As usual when she and my mother got on this subject.

And Mom kept coming back to it like a tongue to a sore tooth. I wasn't sure why. I knew she loved her sister, but she didn't seem to be able to stop herself from constantly poking and prodding at her as if she were a clay statue that wasn't quite dry yet and could still be reshaped. Every now and then, Mom reminded me of Grandma Katz, always wanting everybody to do things *her* way, but I knew Mom would pass out if I ever told her that.

"I know, I know. I'm sorry," Mom said, grabbing the tissue box from the sideboard and slapping it on the table. Unlike Grandma Katz, Mom did usually realize when she'd hurt someone's feelings. "I didn't mean to upset you. I just worry, is all."

"You never *mean* to, but you keep doing it," Gail said, sniffling.

"I'm *sorry*," Mom repeated. "You know I'm a worrywart. At least nursing pays well, and you've been at the hospital long enough to get a daytime schedule. That's all good."

Gail continued to glare at her.

"Let's talk about something else entirely," Mom said. "My problems. Angie's problems." Her mouth curled up on one side as she looked across the table at me.

"I don't have any problems," I said, taking a long slurp of tea and standing up.

"Well, I think there's something you ought to tell your aunt. We can talk about it. You can get her opinion."

"I have homework to do," I said. "Besides, I've had enough opinions for one day."

"What is it, Angie?" Gail wanted to know. She'd wiped her eyes and pulled herself together. "Tell me, honey."

I'd always adored Aunt Gail, and I trusted her not to freak out on me. Still, I was already tired of the moment of revelation, seeing the weird ways people took the news. I was beginning to wish I had a card to pass out to people. Something like I AM TRANSGENDER. FIND OUT WHAT THAT MEANS BEFORE YOU SPEAK TO ME AGAIN. But I sighed and rose to the task. "You know how you said my haircut looks like a boy's?"

She nodded. "Do you want me to shape it up for you? I can make it look more feminine."

Mom let out a little puff of disgusted laughter. "She doesn't want it more feminine. The whole idea is to look like a boy. She's changing her *name*, for God's sake. No more Angela. My daughter is becoming some boy named Grady!" The anger in her voice surprised me. I knew she wasn't happy about my changes, but suddenly she seemed furious.

I couldn't stand it. It wasn't *my* fault this was happening. I was just trying to straighten things out—live the life I was supposed to live. Why was everybody freaking out about it? It was *my* life.

Gail was looking at me, confused. "What's your mother talking about?"

"Aunt Gail, I'm transgender, okay?" I was pretty sure a nurse would know what that meant. "I'm a male, a boy. And I want people to call me Grady, not Angela."

"Oh," she said, looking back and forth from me to Mom. "Well, wow."

"Yeah, wow," Mom said sarcastically. "Big wow. So, every time you think you're having a hard time with that little baby, just remember this is the easy part. Someday he'll be a teenager and all hell will break loose."

"Thanks, Mom," I said quietly. "Thanks for your support. I'm so happy to know that you think of me as a big terrible problem!"

And of course after that I made a fast getaway to my room, punctuating my remarks with the obligatory door slam. I was glad I didn't have to stick around and hear how shocked Aunt Gail was, how she never suspected, and all the rest. I wanted this first part to be over. I wanted Grady to be a real person, for people to know *him*. I wanted to start life over again.

I got the hot-water bottle from the bathroom I shared with Laura and filled it until it bulged. Then I crawled under the covers, hugging that rubber gut-heater as if it were my baby.

Around three o'clock, as I was staring at my Global History book, pretending to read, Mom knocked on my door.

"I'm sorry I got so mad before," she said. "I'm working on how to feel about all this, but it's hard."

"I know," I said. "It's okay."

"Well, it's not okay, but I really came up here to tell you you have a phone call."

"I do?" Eve was the only person who ever called me, and she'd been AWOL for a week or more. Unlike most other high-school kids, I had no cell phone and no need for one. Mom handed me the cordless phone from downstairs.

"Hello?"

"Hey, where did you go? You weren't in TV Production."

"Is this Sebastian?"

"Yeah. I was going to tell you about my Environmental Science project, remember? Stoplight parrotfish?"

Save me.

SEBASTIAN: You wanna come over and see my aquarium? I have two red warthog google-fish and three blue wiggle-whammies! Gosh, fish are so cool!

ME: Sure, Sebastian. I hope your fish have one of those little castles to swim in and out of. That's *really* exciting.

SEBASTIAN: Oh, yeah. I have a castle in the tank—and a mirror in there too, so they can watch themselves going about their busy lives.

ME: And so they get their lipstick on straight.

SEBASTIAN: Ha! Good one!

ME: What do fish do all day, besides eat and poop?

SEBASTIAN: Well, eating and pooping do take up a lot of their time. And dying. Sometimes they do that too.

ME: The old belly-up routine, huh?

SEBASTIAN: Yeah. Oops, just lost another one!

"Are you listening to me?" Sebastian said. "The Smithsonian website says that in lots of fish, gender ambiguity is natural—especially in reef fish. I picked the stoplight parrotfish for my report because they're so pretty, and because they change color when they go from female to male—from dull gray to bright green with a yellow stripe. Isn't that awesome?"

He had my attention now. "What? Fish change from female to male?"

"That's what I'm telling you. Stoplight parrotfish do. Actually all parrotfish do. And the two-banded anemonefish can change either way. Slipper limpets can change back and forth, and so can hamlets and small-eyed goby and water fleas and slime mold—"

"Fleas and slime mold. Wow, I'm in good

company. Does the hamlet fish carry around a skull and ponder suicide?"

Sebastian was quiet for a second. "I thought you'd be interested in this, but it doesn't seem like you are."

I sighed. "It's just . . . I don't know what this has to do with me, Sebastian. I'm not a fish."

"Do you know a lot of other people who were born girls but want to live their lives as boys?"

I had to smile; Sebastian didn't waste words. "No, I don't, but I know there *are* some."

"I'm sure there are, but I thought you'd like some real evidence here that you are not alone in the animal world. There are other living creatures that do this all the time. 'Nature creates many variations.' I'm using that line in my paper."

When you thought of it that way, it did seem kind of amazing. "You're right, Sebastian. I'm sorry I blew you off."

"It's okay," he said, without a trace of hard feelings. "So, do you want to know more?"

"Sure."

"Well, the parrotfish has a beaklike jaw of fused teeth, which is where it gets its name. Besides its regular teeth, it also has a row of sharp ones at the back of its throat—"

"I don't need to know *everything* about it. Just get to the sex part."

He snorted. "Spoken like a real boy, Pinocchio. Okay, some of the parrotfish are born male—those are called primary males. The secondary males are born female, and when they change into males, they're called terminal males or supermales."

"Hey, I like that," I said. "The ones who *change* are supermales—like Superman." I flexed my biceps, not that anyone could see my little muscles pop to attention.

"Well, Superman only changes his clothes, not his gender."

"Okay, okay. Go on."

"The females change into supermales in response to population density; that is, they change when there's a need for more males. The supermales are dominant over the primary males. They apparently get more than their share of the girls."

"Wow. And you just happen to be doing a paper on this fish?"

"Yeah. Life is full of surprises, huh?"

"Tell me about it."

"Are you gonna be in school tomorrow? I'll bring the pictures I got off the Web."

Sound of me plummeting back to earth.

School. Tomorrow. Crap. "Um, I'm not sure about tomorrow. I mean, I'm feeling a little sick."

"Yeah, but staying home isn't going to cure you, is it?"

What a know-it-all. "Sebastian, how come this doesn't throw you like it does everybody else?" I asked him. "Aren't you freaked out by me at all?"

He barked out a laugh. "Are you kidding? I want to be a scientist and a filmmaker. You're, like, my perfect subject!"

"So you're mostly interested in putting me under a microscope." *Great.*

"Or maybe in front of a camera. But that's not the only reason. You know, I liked you before, too. I always thought you were a very cool person."

I thought about that. At least this one weird, geeky little guy thought I was cool. It was a start.

"Okay, I'll meet you at the lockers tomorrow," I said.

"Come early," Sebastian said. "I've got lots of pictures!"

"Hey, Sebastian," I said before he could hang up. "Do you by any chance have an aquarium?"

"Grady," he said, sounding a little hurt, "what do you think I am, a dork?"

Chapter Seven

Tuesday was not much less awful than Monday, especially at the beginning. The news about me seemed to have gotten around the school, and most kids just wanted to stare. People who'd never bothered to glance in my direction before suddenly needed to gawk openly. They studied my walk, they watched my face, they looked for the clues they hadn't picked up before.

I decided not to bring up the subject with my other teachers. My math teacher, Mrs. MacCauley, was about ninety-eight years old and never remembered anybody's name anyway. She usually just pointed at us, although she'd called me both Andrea and Andy a few times, so maybe she was smarter than I thought. Mr. Ludlow, my Global History teacher, called us all by our last names. Being Ms. Katz-McNair had always seemed weird, but becoming *Mr.* Katz-McNair somehow seemed even more bizarre. A mister was a grown man, like Dad, and, although I was happy with the identity of "boy," I wasn't at all sure about making the transition to "man."

Mrs. Norman continued to call me Angela, of course, since no directive had come down from God. Ms. Marino called me Grady, loud and clear, no matter how many groans and giggles issued from the class. And Ms. Unger turned out to be pretty great, or at least as great as somebody who's basically a grouch can be. Not only did she let me use her shower and bathroom, but she told me I could leave a box of pads in there for whenever I needed them.

Which was a big relief. The whole bathroom issue was a much bigger problem than I'd imagined it would be. Before this I probably never used a school bathroom more than once a day, if that, but now, suddenly, I felt like I had to pee all the time. So even though Ms. Unger's office was way the hell on one end of the school and most of my classes were on the other end, it was comforting to know that at least there was someplace I could urinate—or hide out—without fear, even if it meant being late to my next class.

I would talk to Mr. Reed in TV Production about all of this sooner or later, for sure. He was a good guy and I didn't think he'd make a big deal out of it. But of course I wasn't 100 percent sure, and the idea of my favorite class being ruined scared me. As a matter of fact, I was surprised at how much general fear and anxiety lurked inside me these days. I'd never been a fearful person, never even understood phobias like fear of heights or water or snakes or any of those things. And while I knew that my coming out as a transgender person was going to throw certain people for a loop, I somehow hadn't realized how much it would throw me.

I didn't meet people's eyes as I walked down the hall or through the cafeteria. Suddenly, I wasn't raising my hand in class. My legs were shaky as I changed into my gym clothes in Ms. Unger's office, and I jumped at every noise, thinking somebody would come in and see me wearing the binder. And worst of all, as much as I hated to admit it, I was afraid of that damn Danya.

On the plus side, however, was Sebastian. He was waiting for me by our lockers first thing Tuesday morning, notebook in hand. He had enough information about parrotfish to publish a book. I looked through the pictures he'd printed from Internet sites and listened to his excited yakking while the snickering hordes walked behind us. Sebastian didn't even seem to notice them, and having something else to focus on helped me pretend I didn't either.

It turned out that Sebastian also had lunch the same period I did. I'd never noticed him there before, since he liked to sit at a small table in the corner behind a stack of books. And he wasn't one of those kids who read at lunch because no one will sit with them—it's more like no one would sit with him because all he wanted to do was read. I could tell he was making a big sacrifice by asking me to join him.

Sebastian was the only kid I'd ever seen actually eating the hot-lunch choice. He was picking away happily at something called "meatloaf and mashed potatoes" that was drowned in brown goo. I had to move my chair back from the table a little, because the smell of the stuff was enough to make me gag on my hot dog and fries.

"Do you like Stephen Jay Gould?" he asked, picking up the book on the top of his pile.

I shrugged. "Don't know—never read him."

Sebastian's eyes widened. "Really? You have to."

"I'm not much of a science person. I like writing and filmmaking. That's what I really want to do, I think. Write screenplays."

"That would be cool. I want to find a way to use science in my films."

"You mean, like science fiction?"

"More like science fact. Documentaries. But I

like all kinds of movies." He pulled a heavy book from the bottom of his pile. "I got this from the library—have you seen it?"

I took it from him. *Movies of the 90s*. Full of color pictures.

"It's turned me on to some movies I would have missed," he said. "Like *Groundhog Day* and *Being John Malkovich*."

"I've seen *Groundhog Day*," I said. "Bill Murray is great."

Sebastian left his fork standing up in his so-called mashed potatoes and rose off his chair a little bit, stabbing his finger in the air. "I love movies where one little thing is different, and then because of that everything changes. You know what I mean?"

I nodded. Sebastian got more excited about things than anybody else I knew.

"And I also like movies about oddballs. You know, like *Welcome to the Dollhouse* and, oh, *Napoleon Dynamite*! Have you seen that?"

"No."

"I'll rent it for us sometime. You *have* to see it."

All of a sudden a tray smacked me in the back and I felt something cold pouring down my neck. I turned around to see a couple of creeps I didn't even know standing there, collapsing in hysterics.

"Oh, I'm sorry, sir," one of them said. "I seem to have spilled my milk!"

The other one was laughing like a maniac.

I reached back to feel my shirt—sopping wet. *Shit.* And everybody in the vicinity was turning around to see what had happened.

"You're a perfect example of what I was just talking about, Grady," Sebastian continued. "You change one little thing, like your gender, and suddenly all the idiots in the school are too clumsy to carry a tray across the room. Your change has affected everything." He smiled up at Dumb and Dumber as though he'd complimented them.

"What?" They looked confused.

"Grady's shirt is all wet; maybe you could loan him yours?" Sebastian said to one of them.

The guy laughed. "Yeah, right. Like I'd let that pervert wear my clothes."

"It's okay," I mumbled to Sebastian. "Let it go." I knew he was trying to help, but had it occurred to him what would happen if I had to take off my shirt in public? Just because I wanted to live as a boy didn't mean my body had morphed overnight. Was I crazy to bring all this on myself? I'd been practically invisible in this school for more than a year, and now suddenly everybody was talking about me. I knew they were. Talking about private, personal things that were none of their business, imagining what my body looked like, wondering about my sex life. I knew it. I *knew* it. And it was my own fault. I could have kept it a secret longer—until I was out of high school, away from home, where I wouldn't upset my mother and Laura and Eve. I could have just moved somewhere nobody knew me and started all over as a boy.

And then Sebastian was standing up, all five feet of him. Standing up with his puny arms crossed in front of his chest, glaring at my harassers. "What is wrong with you two?" he said loud enough for many onlookers—and there *were* many—to overhear him. "You're acting like six-year-olds—dumping food on somebody because he's different from you!"

One of them laughed. "Hey, that's no *he*; she's just a sicko with penis envy. But maybe that's all you can get, huh, midget?"

Sebastian was red-faced now, and shouting. "I suppose you think *you're* the standard we should all measure ourselves against!"

"Yeah, Kleinhorst," a male voice yelled out. "I wanna be just like you! Ignorant and wasted!" A ripple of laughter swelled around us.

A girl's voice said, "It'll be a sad day when

Kleinhorst and Whitney are our standards of excellence!"

The audience hooted and laughed in agreement.

The idiots didn't know what to do—no one was coming to their defense. The one who seemed to be Kleinhorst dropped the tray with the empty milk glass on our table and pushed past the other guy to walk away, muttering something about not wasting his time with creeps. Whitney, I guess he was, followed.

"Go, Sebastian," the male voice said. "You told those jerks." This time I turned around in time to locate the voice. It belonged to Russ Gallo, a guy from our TV Production class.

Russ was different from the rest of the crew in TV. On the whole the class seemed to attract the less admired high school kids: the skinny, the flabby, the clumsy, the zitty, and now, obviously, the transgender. Maybe because we liked hiding out behind the camera, I don't know. But anyway, Russ Gallo didn't fit the stereotype. He wasn't an Adonis, but he was a good-looking, happy guy who seemed to have a million friends. Although apparently not Kleinhorst or Whitney.

He walked over to where Sebastian and I were sitting, pulling a blue denim shirt out of his backpack.

"Hey, I've got an extra shirt," he said. "I brought it yesterday for my cable interview with the band teacher. Mr. Reed said I couldn't just wear a T-shirt. You can give it back to me in class one of these days."

"Thanks," I said, taking the shirt from him.

"Don't let those idiots get to you, man. They're brain-dead."

I didn't know what to say. Russ Gallo was acting like I was a normal person.

I hadn't noticed someone else walking up behind him until she said, "I heard you changed your name. What is it now?"

And there stood Kita Charles, Russ Gallo's amazingly beautiful girlfriend, speaking to me.

"Um, well, I haven't changed it legally . . . yet. But I'm going by the name of Grady now."

She nodded. "Grady. I like it. There's 'gray' in it—my favorite color."

I was amazed. She *got* it. But I didn't say anything; I couldn't. Kita Charles was looking into my eyes and I was looking back into hers, and that was distracting my brain from coming up with words. I know it sounds crazy because I'd never even spoken to her before, but I'd always thought of Kita as someone kind of like me. She was biracial—Japanese and African-American was what I'd heard—which made her stand out in our mostly white school. Her skin was like polished oak and she wore her long black hair in dreads. What fascinated me about Kita was that her identity, like mine, wasn't simple. There was nobody else like her at Buxton High; she was unique. You couldn't figure her out just by looking.

Russ looked at her quizzically. "Gray is your favorite color? *Gray?* It's not even a color!"

Kita sighed and smiled at me. "Oh, Russell," she said. "Sometimes you are so totally normal, I can't believe you're my boyfriend."

Chapter Eight

I asked Sebastian if he wanted to come home with me after school, mostly because I didn't want to walk home alone. He probably knew that, but he came anyway. I'd forgotten to warn him that we were going to Santa's Village, and his mouth dropped open when he saw which yard I was turning into.

"Wait," he said. "You live *here*?"

"Well, somebody has to," I said.

"Oh my God," he said, turning in circles to take it all in. "We used to come here. When I was little. I remember that Santa stuffed into the chimney and those teddy bears and that—"

"I know, I know. We're part of everybody's magical childhood memories," I said, waiting for him to laugh at it all with me. He didn't.

"The Barbies are still here too!" he said, pointing.

Obviously, nobody ever forgets the Barbies. "So were you ever here at night?" I asked. "When the curtains were open?"

I could tell he was sorting through forgotten images. His face lit up. "Yeah! You could see right inside the house! There was a toy train, and a whole bunch of presents, and an old guy in a funny smashed hat who came around and lit the fireplaces!"

"The old guy was my dad."

He smacked me on the arm. "You are so lucky!"

"You are *so* out of your mind."

As we walked inside, Sebastian fingered the fake icicles hanging over the back door as if they'd been placed there by Jolly Old St. Nick himself. It was practically unheard of for me to bring any friends home except Eve, so I expected Mom to greet Sebastian with great relief and celebration. I was unaware, however, that there were several crises currently unfolding in the Katz-McNair household which were demanding all her attention.

Before we could see her, we could hear Laura screaming, "Make him stop it!" while Charlie drummed his fists on the kitchen counter and sang in an off-key tenor.

"The dogs crawl in, the dogs crawl out, the dogs play pig knuckles on your snout."

"It's 'pinochle,' not 'pig's knuckles,'" Mom

said as she applied a goopy white cream to Laura's left knee and elbow. "Pinochle is a card game."

"Mom!" Laura choked out her words. "He's saying 'dogs' and it's 'worms'! *Worms* crawl in, *worms* crawl out—not *dogs*!" It was then that I noticed the purple eye shadow and black mascara dripping down my sister's face.

"What happened to you?" I asked her.

But Charlie kept up his refrain, getting louder and louder. "They eat your eyes, they eat your nose, they eat the jelly between your toes. A big green dog with rolling eyes, crawls in your stomach and out your eyes."

"Make him stop!" Laura shrieked, and then she began to sob.

"Your stomach turns a slimy green, and pus pours out like whipping cream—"

"Stop singing that silly song," Mom said. "Your sister's going crazy, and I'm not far behind her."

"I'm going to keep singing until I get a dog!" Charlie said. "I don't see why I can't have a dog!"

"First of all, I'm allergic to dogs," Mom said. She slapped a big piece of gauze on Laura's arm and began to tape it down. "And secondly, I'm not taking care of a dog now, on top of everything else."

"I'll take care of it—I promise! I need *something* to play with!" Charlie said. "How about a hamster?"

"No, Charlie!"

Sebastian took it all in with amazement. I couldn't have written a better scene myself.

"Did you fall down?" I asked Laura, trying again.

She stopped crying and raised a furious face toward me. "Oh, right, act like you're all concerned about me. Like it's not all your fault."

"Laura, it's not your sister's . . . I mean, your . . ." Mom gave up and sighed. "Oh, I don't know. Maybe it's all my fault."

"Are you going to tell me what happened to Laura?" I asked Mom this time.

"She fell down on the way home. She was running, and there was a tree root, and she didn't see it—"

Laura interrupted Mom's calm explanation to give me her version of events. "I was running because Mira and Sarah and Brit and everybody I've ever *met* want to ask me questions about my weird sister, and I don't know what to tell them. I was running home because I'm humiliated that the entire school knows I'm related to the most bizarre person they've ever heard of. *That's* why I fell down."

Fortunately, I didn't have to answer this charge immediately, because Charlie started to sing again. "Found a puppy, found a puppy, found a puppy just now. I just now found a puppy, found a puppy just now. Had a worm in it, had a worm in it—"

"I hate you! All of you!" Laura sobbed as she ran from the kitchen.

"Charlie, be quiet," Mom demanded. "I have enough on my mind without—"

"If I can't have a dog, then I should at least be allowed to go to a regular middle school next year instead of being stuck at home, just me and Daniel and our mothers every day. It's *boring*."

Mom turned her back on him and only then did she see that I had someone with me. "Oh dear, I didn't realize . . ."

"This is Sebastian Shipley. He's in my TV Production class," I told her.

Sebastian stuck out his small hand. "Nice to meet you, Mrs. Katz-McNair."

I could tell she was surprised by this polite miniature person. "It's nice to meet you too, Sebastian," she said, giving his hand a half-hearted shake. "I'm sorry you had to walk in on this scene. Laura's very emotional these days, and every little thing seems to set her off."

"Well, I guess having your sister suddenly become your brother might not seem like a little thing to her."

Mom looked sort of pale; she obviously wasn't

getting any more comfortable with my new gender as the days went by.

"Are you two hungry?" she asked, deftly changing the subject.

But before we could reply, Charlie interrupted again. "You don't understand anything! I *need* a dog! I swear to God I'm getting myself a dog. I'll go to a shelter and get one by myself! I swear to God!"

"You're not swearing to *anybody*, do you hear me?" It took Mom awhile to lose her temper, especially with Charlie, but once the point was reached, there was no going back. Her voice careened into the soprano range and blew right into Charlie's face. "You're going to your room, and you'll stay there until I tell you to come out! And I don't want to hear a word about it!"

I motioned to Sebastian to follow me back outside.

"Whoa! Some family!" he said as if he were complimenting me.

"Not like yours?"

He snorted. "My mother never raises her voice—it gives her a headache. But then, she never really has to. I mean, I'm the only kid, and I'm damn near perfect."

"I'm sure. She never argues with your dad?"

"Not in living memory," he said. "He works about twelve hours a day, so he's not around that much. He's a big-deal lawyer."

"I guess he makes a lot of money."

Sebastian shrugged. "I guess. But making money is stupid. I mean, you have to make *some* money, but I want to do something that actually matters when I'm an adult. Otherwise, why bother to *be* an adult? Just so you can buy stuff?"

This was not the kind of conversation I was used to having with anyone. But I enjoyed this kid, I really did. I liked the way I never knew what was going to come out of his mouth next. So I decided to broach the topic I'd been thinking about since lunchtime.

"That was really cool the way Russ Gallo came over and gave me his shirt," I said, sneaking up on my real topic of interest. "I've never even spoken to him before."

"Yeah, Russ is a good guy. You know, I was thinking, if you're gonna be a boy now, maybe you oughta get some more muscles. Like, work out or something. So if people push you around, you can push back."

I shrugged. "Not really too interested in muscles."

He grabbed my upper arm between his thumb and first finger. "Pretty skimpy for a guy."

"You should talk!"

"Hey, nobody spilled milk on *me* today!"

I dragged the conversation back to my original direction. "I thought Russ's girlfriend seemed nice too," I said.

"Kita? I guess. I don't know her very well," Sebastian said. My heart had begun to sputter when he said her name out loud. Kita Charles. I'd never heard a more beautiful name.

"So, have they been together for a long time or what?"

"I think so. Since last year anyway."

"Huh. That's pretty long for high school."

Sebastian shrugged.

"I mean, you know, Kita's so pretty. You'd think she'd be dating lots of different guys."

Sebastian stopped walking and looked over at me. "What? Do you like Kita?"

"No!" I yelled. "God, where'd you get that idea? I was just asking how long—"

"Okay, okay, don't get your panties in a twist."

The fear that seized me when Sebastian made his correct guess came out of nowhere. I wasn't expecting him to figure me out, and I wasn't expecting myself to flip out about it. But what if he told somebody that I liked Kita? It would be bad enough if I were just the school lesbian—imagine the hoopla that would ensue now that I was out as transgender! If Kita knew I liked her like *that*, she'd probably be as disgusted as everybody else. Everybody but goofy Sebastian.

"God, Sebastian," I continued, trying to calm my racing heart. "Just because I asked you a simple question about somebody—"

"Look, I don't care if you like her. Kita's a beautiful girl, and she's nice, too. I wouldn't blame you for liking her."

"Well, I *don't*, okay? Not the way you mean."

We didn't speak for a few minutes after that. We were wandering aimlessly down the hill by my house, and I was trying to think of an excuse to go home without Sebastian following me, when I noticed who was coming up the hill toward us. "Turn here!" I said, taking Sebastian's arm and pulling him around the corner and ten yards down the block where we'd no longer be visible to the approaching party.

"What are we doing?" Sebastian looked expectant.

"There are some girls coming up the hill. They're going to Eve Patrick's house, and I . . . well, I don't want her to see me. Especially when she's with *them*."

"Who's *them*?" he whispered conspiratorially.

"These girls she hangs around with now—

Danya somebody, and Melanie and Zoe. Danya's a real jerk."

Sebastian nodded. "Danya Seifert," he said. "Known her since elementary school. She's a big bully."

I grunted. "I guess so. I don't usually think of girls as bullies."

"Not all girls are alike, as you know."

I shook my head. "I don't get it. Why does Eve even want to hang around with her? There must be other girls who'd be nicer to her."

"They all want to be Danya's friend," Sebastian said. "Because if you aren't her friend, you could be her enemy. And believe me, that's a lot worse."

"The awful thing is that being around these creeps is turning Eve into a creep too."

"She used to be a good friend, huh?" Sebastian said. If your IQ was based on how well you guessed personal stuff about other people, this guy would be a genius. Actually, he probably *was* a genius.

"My best friend. Now we hardly speak."

He nodded, then paced quietly back toward the corner.

I followed. "Don't let them see you!"

"I just want to listen," he said.

They stopped in front of Eve's house. It wasn't

hard to hear them, especially Danya, whose voice was like a trumpet.

"I just don't get how you could *ever* be friends with her. Or *it*, or whatever. Didn't you know she was a pervert?"

I think Eve answered her, but her voice was too quiet to hear.

"If I was like that, I'd just go ahead and kill myself. I really would. I couldn't stand to be such a sicko. I'm telling you, Eve, if I find out you spoke to that deviant, even once—and I *will* find out if you do—you will be very sorry. In fact, you'll regret it for a long time!"

Suddenly I felt dizzy, and my legs wobbled a little. Danya thought I ought to *kill* myself? Jesus, I didn't even know this girl, and she wanted me dead! The worst I'd ever wished on her was that her mouth be magically sewn shut for a week or two. And she also seemed to be threatening Eve. My stomach was suddenly sour with guilt. Had I put my former best friend into this awful situation? Or had she done it to herself? Why did she want to be friends with Danya to begin with?

Sebastian snorted, and before I could stop him, he was going around the corner, heading toward the girls. "No!" I said, but it was too late.

"I couldn't help overhearing you, Danya," he said as he walked up to the group.

She swiveled around and glared at him. "Where'd you come from, Tiny Tim?"

He ignored that and said, "I was just wondering if you might be talking about my friend Grady." He gestured toward the corner, and all four girls looked in my direction. *Crap.* I could run away and hope they hadn't already seen me, but that seemed more cowardly than the situation demanded. I could walk around the corner as if I'd just been headed in that direction anyway, which no one would believe for a second, but at least there'd be no chance for them to watch my sorry butt retreating down the street like a whipped puppy.

I sauntered around the corner. *Damn you, Sebastian Shipley.*

Danya's face pulled itself in tight as if I had a skunk in my pocket. "What are *you* doing here?"

"I live here. Over there," I said, pointing in the general direction of Peace and Joy.

Zoe sucked in a big breath. "Oh, it's the Christmas House! You live in the Christmas House?"

I nodded.

"I always loved that place," she said, smiling. Until she caught a glimpse of Danya's glowering mug.

"Are you *speaking* to it?" she asked Zoe.

Zoe's face turned white. "No! I was just surprised! I didn't know—"

"Well, shut up," Danya ordered. Zoe clamped her lips together and looked down at the sidewalk.

"I always loved Grady's house when I was a kid too," Sebastian said, as if we were all having a normal conversation. "I always thought, *Wow, whoever goes to all that trouble just to make kids happy must be really great. I bet a wonderful family lives there.*"

Danya glared at him. "Are you under the impression that we give a damn what you think?"

But Sebastian babbled on. "See, it's this thing about you calling my friend Grady a pervert, when really he's just a transgender person. Which is not all that unusual, actually. If you were interested in doing some research, there are lots of sites on the Internet—"

"Believe me, shorty, I'm not in the least interested. Get lost, both of you."

"But what really bothers me," Sebastian continued in the same calm voice, "is you telling Grady's friend here that she can't talk to him. As if you're in charge of everybody."

Eve had been keeping her eyes carefully focused on the picket fence around her house, but when Sebastian said that about me being her friend, her head twitched and she looked up at Danya. "He's not . . . she's not . . . I mean . . . we aren't friends anymore! We really aren't!"

I wasn't sure if I was saying it to save Eve or to

save my own self-respect, but I said it loud enough for the entire neighborhood to hear. "She's right, Danya. We're not friends. I would never be friends with anybody who hung around with a soul-sucking bitch like you."

Right then I wished I had those muscles Sebastian had mentioned earlier, because, pacifist though I'd always been, at that moment I really wanted to bounce Danya Seifert on the sidewalk like a basketball and see if the crap would fall out of her head.

Sebastian must have realized I'd hit my boiling point. He took me gently by the arm and pulled me away from the girls.

"Must be going," he said. "Nice to chat with you."

Danya was snorting like a bull, but I was only looking at Eve. Just before I turned around and walked away she looked up at me, and there in her eyes I could see that scared kid lurking, the one who could never stand for anyone to be mad at her, especially me.

Chapter Nine

I managed to wait until we'd put a block of houses and a row of tall maple trees between us and them before I lit into Sebastian. "For Christ's sake, why did you do that? I told you I didn't want to talk to them!"

"Well, I *did*," Sebastian said. "You can't just ignore people like Danya. She won't stop being a creep unless people call her on it."

"You think she cares what *we* think of her? Besides, she probably likes being called a soul-sucking bitch."

"Possibly. Still, you can't let her walk all over you."

"Maybe she's just saying what everybody else is thinking." I wondered if that was really true; were there other people who thought I should off myself so their world wouldn't be soiled by my presence? I hunched up my shoulders the way I used to when I first started getting breasts and didn't want anyone to notice. Eventually my neck and back would start to hurt, but in the meantime, I felt invisible. "I should never have told anybody. There's no place I can go now and feel good. Feel safe. At home they're all upset, at school everybody's freaking out . . . I have to walk half a mile to use a bathroom so no one is offended by me. People stare at me everywhere I go. I can't stand being a freak anymore."

Sebastian was quiet for a minute, while I tensed my jaw and ground my teeth to powder. Then he said. "You'll get used to it."

"Get *used* to it? What are you talking about?"

He shrugged. "Look at me. I'm Tiny Tim. You get used to stuff. You don't really want to keep pretending you're somebody you aren't, do you? Although, if you do, I'll take you to the Winter Carnival dance."

I knew he was trying to joke me out of feeling bad, but I didn't say anything. I could feel Danya's words eating into my soul. Why hadn't I realized what a huge deal this was going to turn out to be? I guess I'd just been thinking about it for so long that I forgot changing your gender was not even a question for most people. They just took for granted being a boy or a girl. I couldn't imagine what it would be like to be so sure of yourself. To be scornful of anybody who wasn't just like you.

We'd walked all the way to the Four Corners strip mall by then, kicking rocks and road trash as we shuffled along.

"I'm gonna stop into Atkins Pharmacy before I go home," Sebastian said. "They have this organic peppermint shampoo I like."

I stared at him. "You use organic peppermint shampoo?"

"Yeah. What do you use?"

"Whatever my mother buys and leaves in the shower."

He shook his head. "You should try this stuff. It makes your head tingle."

I put my hand up in the stop position. "Tingle? Too much information." But I followed him into the store anyway, since I had nowhere else to go.

Sebastian couldn't immediately find his beloved shampoo on its usual shelf. Then a sales clerk, an overweight, middle-aged woman with a mouthful of gum, came up behind us. "Can I help you boys find something?"

I was almost afraid to turn around and face her. She'd called me a boy. What if she realized her mistake and got embarrassed and . . . I couldn't take it. Not today.

"I'm looking for that organic peppermint

shampoo you sell," Sebastian said. "It's usually right here."

"Follow me," she said, poking a finger into her breastbone. "Wilma knows where everything is. We moved all the organic stuff into one section." She walked a few aisles down and stopped in front of a sign that said ALL-NATURAL ORGANIC PRODUCTS.

"I don't know what makes some of 'em organic and some of 'em not," she said. "Is this what you want?" She held up a green bottle.

"Yes! Thank you! That's it!" You'd think Sebastian had found gold.

"How come you like it so much?" Wilma asked.

"It smells good," Sebastian said. "And it makes your head tingle."

"Yeah? Maybe I'll try it," she said. "I bet your girlfriends like it, huh?" She smiled right into my face and winked at me.

I tried to smile back, but I could feel the corners of my mouth quivering. It appeared that this woman actually thought I was a boy.

Sebastian took his shampoo up to the counter, and Wilma rang up the sale. I had to know for sure. I looked around the nearby shelves for an item with which to test her. When Sebastian stepped aside, I put a can of shaving cream on the counter. Not that girly stuff Laura uses to shave her legs, but a black can with a big ship on it. Why, I wondered, were ships for men? They should put a lawn mower on it, or, better yet, a jockstrap.

Wilma chewed her gum nonchalantly as she rang up my sale, took my money, put the shaving cream in a plastic bag, and handed it over. "There you go, sir," she said, still grinning. "Have a nice day!"

I followed Sebastian out of the store. "Did she call you sir?" I asked him.

"Maybe. Can't remember." Then his face brightened. "Did she call *you* sir?"

I nodded my head, feeling—stupidly—as if I might cry if I tried to speak.

"Well, my friend, you passed," he said, putting a hand on my back. "You are now officially a boy."

By the time I got back home, it was almost dark. Dad had just switched on two billion megawatts of electricity. Jesus and Rudolph glowed, Barbies skated, and plastic carolers started listing all the crap their true loves gave to them.

"Hey, kiddo," he greeted me. "Can you give me a hand carrying in some firewood?"

"Sure," I said. "I don't have to put on a costume though, do I?"

He laughed. "You kids. I think I enjoy this more than you do!" He *thinks?* "Just help me stack it by the back door. I have to get my own costume on before I build any fires."

We tramped out through the backyard to our property line, where a cord of wood had been stacked to get us through the holidays. "Dad, do you think . . . I mean, how long do we have to . . ." There just wasn't a good way to ask him. "The thing is, none of us kids believe in Santa Claus anymore, so you don't have to go to all this trouble for us."

He looked back at me, confused. "But it's fun, isn't it? You don't have to believe in Santa Claus to enjoy the decorations! Besides, it's no trouble for me—I enjoy it."

What could I say? The guy liked to wear dumb clothes and make a spectacle of himself. I gave up.

We piled up enough wood for two or three nights of blazing nineteenth-century fires before Mom called us in for dinner. I was really not anxious to sit across the table from Laura and those accusing eyes with the runny makeup. I guess Dad heard my deep sigh.

"Problems?" he asked, but I knew he didn't really want to know. Dad always pretended there was nothing wrong with his kids; he called it looking on the bright side. Even if you were barfing on the carpet, he'd say, "She doesn't look sick to me!" His theory was that if you didn't dwell on problems, they'd just disappear. Or Mom would take care of them and he could continue to believe we didn't have any.

"Not really," I said. It seemed okay to lie to somebody who didn't really want to know the truth anyway.

Dad cleared his throat and surprised me for a change. "If it's about this name-changing thing . . . well, I want you to know that you're still my kid, and I love you, no matter what your name is." He slapped me on the shoulder.

"Thanks, Dad." I stood looking at the kitchen door but didn't open it. "But, you know, it's not just the name that's changed. It's that . . . I'm different than everybody thought."

"You're still my kid, aren't you?" He laughed uneasily.

"Yeah, but now I'm your son instead of your daughter."

He looked at me, really looked at me, and said, "Truth is, it doesn't surprise me that much. Not that I was expecting it, you understand. Just that, in a way you've always been my son. You know what I mean?"

I sort of did know. He meant that we liked to do the same kinds of things—"guy" stuff that Mom and Laura didn't care about. But was that what made me a boy? Charlie was a boy too, and he didn't give a damn about cars or carpentry projects. I was pretty sure he'd never held a hammer in his hands. So what did it mean that I felt like a boy? If I couldn't really put it into words myself, was it fair that I was making Laura and Mom and Eve suffer for it?

And yet, hadn't I been suffering for a long time now? Every time the swimming teacher had said, "Boys line up here, girls over there," I'd had to think consciously about which line I should stand in. I'd wanted to play soccer on the boys' team when I was nine, but I wasn't allowed to, so I stopped playing altogether. Or, worst, the times Mom had forced me to wear a dress with a lacy collar and a ribbon at the waist to visit Grandma Katz in the nursing home. The dress made me feel like a fool. I didn't want fancy white ankle socks and Mary Janes. I wanted to wear crew socks and sneakers like Charlie did. Because I knew that that was the kind of person I was: a crew-socks-wearing person, not an ankle-socks-wearing person. And maybe if people didn't divide everybody up into just two groups—male and female, two lines only—I could have just *been* a crew-socks-wearing person who played on the boys' soccer team and it would have been okay. I wouldn't have had to make a big deal out of being a boy, which seemed to be the part that was making a lot of people crazy.

Dinner was not fun, but at least it was quiet. We were jammed around the small kitchen table, of course, since the dining room was now a stage, but we did our best not to make physical contact with each other. Charlie was mad at Mom for actually disciplining him for a change; he picked angrily at his stew and only ate the meat out of it. Laura seemed to be eating only vegetables these days; the two of them could have shared one bowl instead of wasting two halves. By the glares Laura was sending across the table, you would have thought I was the one who butchered the cow. Mom and Dad just looked tired.

I, however, ate everything that was put in front of me, like a good boy, loaded the dishwasher, and disappeared into my room. The phone rang almost immediately, and Mom called upstairs to say it was for me.

I figured it must be Sebastian, since no one else seemed to be speaking to me. "Hello?" I waited.

"Hello? Who is this?" I thought I was being pranked and was about to hang up when I heard the voice, small and frightened.

"Don't hang up. It's me."

Eve. I took the phone away from my ear and held the handset over the cradle, as if she could see this empty threat, then put it back to my ear.

"Are you there, Angela?"

Angela. She didn't even intend to try. "Give me one good reason why I shouldn't hang up on you," I said.

She was quiet for a few seconds. "I don't have one," she finally said. "I just wanted to say I'm sorry you heard what Danya said this afternoon, and to tell you that I didn't really mean it about not being your friend anymore."

"You didn't?"

"No! I had to say that. If I didn't, Danya wouldn't have been *my* friend anymore!"

I rolled my eyes even though no one was around to see. "Do you honestly think that Danya is your friend, Eve?"

She sighed. "I know she doesn't act like she is, but she lets me hang around with her."

"Why do you *want* to hang around with her? She's the meanest person I've ever met!"

"Yeah, but if she likes you, then she isn't so

mean. Besides, now everybody knows that I'm Danya's friend. Which kind of makes me *somebody*."

"And if everybody knew you were my friend, what would that make you—nobody?"

Silence.

I wished I could reach through the telephone and shake Eve. What was wrong with her? Didn't our friendship mean anything to her anymore? "Danya thinks I ought to kill myself," I said. "Is that what everybody else thinks too?"

"No! Oh, Angela, no! Nobody thinks that. Danya just says crazy stuff like that because . . . I don't know . . . I guess because everybody pays attention to her. You wouldn't really do that, would you?"

"Gee, much as I'd love to get on Danya's good side, I don't think I'll go that far."

"Good," Eve said. "I mean, I didn't think you would, just . . . well, that would be terrible, Angela."

"Grady," I reminded her. "It would sure piss off Her Highness if she knew you were talking to me on the phone right now, wouldn't it?"

"You aren't going to—you wouldn't tell her, would you?" I could imagine the tears pooling in the corners of Eve's eyes, but she wasn't going to cry her way into my sympathy this time.

"I just hope it's worth it, Eve."

"Worth *what*?" she asked, her voice trembling.

"I hope being Danya's friend is worth losing my friendship."

"But I told you—I *am* still your friend. I just can't hang around with you anymore."

"See, Eve, the thing is . . . I *did* mean what I said this afternoon. I'm not your friend anymore—and you aren't mine. A friend would have stood up for me when Danya called me a sicko and suggested I off myself. You didn't."

I hung up the phone quietly, knowing that Eve was probably bawling her eyes out. I wished I didn't care.

Chapter Ten

For the next week or so the only way I could endure my daily life was to make up scenes in which I imagined all the rotten things people were saying behind my back. For example, in the teachers' lunchroom:

MRS. NORMAN: [chowing down on a microwaved veggie burger] I told Angela I'm not changing any names on any permanent records. That's a decision for the principal to make.

DR. RIDGEWAY: [delicately squirting canned cheese onto a Wheat Thin] I told her I'd need to talk to her parents first. Pass the buck to them. Whole thing is probably their fault anyway. We had a kid here a few years ago who wanted to be a girl, remember? Turned out his parents were divorced; father lived in another state. Kid was all screwed up.

MS. MARINO: [sipping her Diet Dew] I'm trying to help Grady become empowered and take pride in him . . . her . . . himself, but I don't really know how. I mean, I've never met a . . . you know . . . one of those . . . a person like that before.

MS. UNGER: [knocking back a large coffee, black] "Transgender" is the word you're looking for. And divorce does not cause gender dysphoria, Dr. Ridgeway. If it did, we'd have a few hundred kids like Grady.

MRS. MACCAULEY: [pecking at a ginger-snap cookie] Who's this Grady?

MS. UNGER: Listen, people. If you want to do the kid a favor, don't mention this in front of Coach Speranza. What a bigot.

MRS. MACCAULEY: I don't believe I know anyone named Jenny Dysphoria, do I?

COACH SPERANZA: [wolfing down his third wife-made sandwich] Hello? I'm sitting right here, sweetie pie!

MS. UNGER: Oops. Guess I'm getting pretty good at ignoring you.

COACH SPERANZA: This about that girl that looks like a boy? What's wrong with her anyway?

DR. RIDGEWAY: She's just a confused lesbian, that's all.

COACH SPERANZA: [snorting] Any lesbian is a confused lesbian, dontcha think?

MRS. NORMAN: [shuddering] If only these children could get their minds on something wholesome. Sex, sex, sex—that's all they're interested in.

MS. UNGER: What were you interested in at their age? Crossword puzzles?

MRS. NORMAN: [unwrapping a Twinkie] I read lit-er-a-ture.

MS. MARINO: [scraping the bottom of her yogurt container] I'm a people person. I've always wanted to make a difference in the world.

MS. UNGER: What makes you think Buxton is part of the world?

I couldn't stop hearing the voices as I walked down the hallways, slumped at my desk, or sat in the cafeteria. I imagined that everyone was talking about me. More than once I caught Laura picking at her lunch and glaring at me over the tops of her friends' heads.

LAURA: I think Angela's just doing this to hurt

me. Because I'm prettier than she is. And I know how to wear makeup.

MIRA: You think so? Maybe we should do an intervention! Like on TV! We could hold her down and do a makeover on her!

BRIT: Like on *Extreme Makeover*!

SARAH: Yeah, but I can't help you because I'm not allowed to come over to your house anymore because your sister is a pervert and all.

BRIT: What's weird about *Extreme Makeover* is that all the people end up looking sort of the same.

MIRA: But Sarah, if we make Angela a real girl, she won't *be* a pervert anymore.

LAURA: [shaking her head, hopelessly] She'll never let you do it. Besides, who would we get to hold her down? She's taller than any of us.

BRIT: How about that Kleinhorst guy? He's big, and I hear he *hates* her. He'd probably do it.

SARAH: We'd have to get all new makeup, though. I mean, I wouldn't use *my* stuff on a queer—I'd have to throw it all away afterward.

MIRA: Why? You think Angela has cooties?

LAURA: I think Angela has a mental illness. Why is she doing this to me?

Oh yeah, I made up a few involving Eve, too, but they were even more depressing. Besides, Eve's good buddy Danya said what she thought right to my face, so I didn't have to imagine it.

I ended up not coming out to Mr. Reed, but I think he knew anyway. How could he not? He was a smart guy and not deaf or blind. I kept trying to decide if he was treating me any differently, but, if he was, he was only nicer. And then I wondered if *that* should make me mad too, but you can't just go around being mad at everybody all the time. It's exhausting.

"The assignment sheets are up for December—we've got two shoots together!" Sebastian said when I walked into TV class one afternoon. "First we're taping the chorus concert Friday night."

I groaned.

"Hey, it's better than another basketball game. All those giants with long, skinny legs and size fifteen feet."

I could see Sebastian's point.

"Besides," he whispered, "Kita Charles is in the chorus!"

I whipped my head in circles to make sure Russ Gallo wasn't standing near enough to hear.

"Will you shut up about her?" I whispered back. "I told you I'm not—"

"Yeah, I know what you told me. I also know what I know. Every time somebody says her name, your face lights up like a jack-o'-lantern."

"Sebastian, *please*," I begged.

"And you'll be interested to know that I heard her and Russ arguing this morning before my math class, which, by the way, Kita is in. We're becoming quite friendly."

"Where's the list?" I asked, turning away from him.

He followed me to the bulletin board where Mr. Reed had tacked up the new assignment sheets.

"You have to work tomorrow morning's assembly, too," Sebastian pointed out. "With Russ."

"So? I like doing assemblies. I get out of part of the classes right before and after."

"It's a basketball assembly."

"I know. You have to go too—everybody does."

"Yeah, but I can sleep through it," Sebastian said.

"Sleep? Through all that cheerleader noise—the whooping and screaming?"

"Well, I can close my eyes, anyway." He pointed at a spot farther down on the second page. "Did you see this? We're going to the dance together after all!"

There it was: DECEMBER 23, WINTER CARNIVAL DANCE: RUSSELL GALLO, SEBASTIAN SHIPLEY, GRADY KATZ-MCNAIR.

Wait a minute. GRADY KATZ-MCNAIR. Why hadn't I noticed that before? I slid my eyes back to my other two listings. Yup, Grady.

"I never said anything to Mr. Reed about calling me Grady. Did you?"

"I think I mentioned it to him," Sebastian said.

"You *mentioned* it to him?"

He turned his palms skyward in the universal gesture for "What's your problem?" "He heard some of the other teachers talking about it, and he asked me if you were changing your name. So I told him."

"Did you tell him *why* I was changing it?"

"Grady, I don't think that's much of a secret anymore."

Another thing occurred to me. "Did you ask him to put us on the crew for the Winter Carnival?"

He looked away. "I might have—"

"Mentioned it. Jesus, Sebastian, are you running my life now?"

"Well, somebody has to! Besides, it'll be fun!"

I groaned. "You have an odd idea of fun. Watching a bunch of teenagers doll up and dance at the country club, pretending to be grown-ups. I bet Russ is mad. He was probably planning to take Kita to the dance."

"Yeah, I'm a little bummed," came a voice from behind me. I shuddered. Thank God Sebastian hadn't made some crack about me liking Kita with Russ standing right there.

"But Kita will go with her friends, and I'll take some breaks to dance with her. She won't care that much—she'd rather talk than dance anyway."

"So, we'll have three cameras at the dance," Sebastian said. "We should be able to get some great footage."

"What great footage? It's just people dancing. And not very well either, I would guess. Does anybody even watch these videos afterward?" I asked. I wasn't sure why, but I was suddenly in a very pissy mood. "I mean, don't you sometimes feel like you're wasting your time taping all these silly events?"

"The Winter Carnival dance is not silly!" Sebastian said, clearly irritated.

Russ laughed. "Well, it is kind of silly, but the girls like it. And I like the girls. Especially when they're dressed to kill."

Girls, plural? Or just Kita? If Kita dressed to kill, I just might die.

"And for your information, Grady, lots of people

watch the local cable channel. My mother's cousin is constantly telling me how much she enjoys it," Sebastian said.

Oh, well then, that made it all worthwhile. Sebastian's mother's cousin was watching.

Russ put a hand on my shoulder. "So, Grady, I guess we're doing the assembly tomorrow. That should be okay. Word is that George Garrison and Ben London have some secret plan to kick it into high gear. Should be funny."

"Yeah? Great." Russ was acting almost as if we were friends now, which I really appreciated. Actually, it picked my whole mood up. Not that I minded having only one, tiny, goofball friend, but having a second, more or less normal one couldn't be a bad thing.

"I'll meet you here at quarter to ten to get the equipment!" he said as he walked away.

"I'll be here!" I called back, smiling perhaps too hugely.

Sebastian noticed. "Calm down. You're just taping an assembly with him, not dating him. Or his girlfriend."

I turned a blistering look on him. "Stop saying stuff about Kita."

He shook his head. "Wow. You're crazy about her, aren't you?"

I bent down to hiss in his ear. "What difference would it make if I was? Kita Charles is not interested in someone like me. So shut up about it!"

But, of course he didn't. "Why wouldn't she be interested in you? She could be. You're very good-looking, you know. Actually, you're better looking as a guy than you were as a girl."

"What? How do you know? You aren't a girl." Even though I pretended Sebastian didn't know what he was talking about, now that he'd pronounced me good-looking, I was hanging on his words.

"I have eyes, don't I? I'm saying, you always looked good, but now that you're a boy you just seem more comfortable with yourself, and that makes you more attractive."

"You think I'm attractive?" The begging was getting a little bit pathetic, I know.

"Hey, I asked you to the Winter Carnival dance, didn't I?" Sebastian shook his head at my obtuseness and walked away. I still wasn't convinced though. After all, Sebastian was not a regular person—he got excited about parrotfish.

The assembly started out just like all sports assemblies: A herd of cheerleaders clad in blue miniskirts and white turtlenecks with BUXTON (which always looked like BUXOM to me) written across their chests in blue script came tumbling out onto the gymnasium floor, their sneakers seemingly spring-loaded, chanting and yelling all the way. Their excitement was echoed by the crowd stuffed into the bleachers, who hooted so loudly that you could barely understand the words to the cheers. *Sleep tight, Sebastian.*

Mr. Reed had told Russ and me to bring just one camera, since we wouldn't have to get any fancy angle shots. You didn't really need two people to do a job like this, but Mr. Reed always sent us in pairs so if somebody goofed up or forgot something, there'd still be a decent chance the other person wasn't as big a dope and the whole shoot wouldn't be ruined. We set up the tripod and camera halfway up the bleachers at a spot over a doorway so nobody was in front of us, and we connected our equipment into the microphone down on the gym floor so we wouldn't pick up only audience noise.

I happened to see Kita walk into the gym with a group of her girlfriends. She knew Russ would be filming, of course, and she scanned the bleachers until her gaze landed on us. She waved.

"There's Kita!" I told Russ.

He'd been focusing the camera, but he looked up briefly, saw her, and waved back. I figured once he'd done it, it was okay for me to wave too. The girls found seats on the lower bleachers, and Kita turned back to them. It was too bad I'd seen where she was sitting, because from then on it was almost impossible to keep my eyes from drifting in that direction.

Dr. Ridgeway stood up to give his usual brief "Fight, fight, fight" speech, which always seemed ironic, since normally he's the one telling everybody *not* to fight. When he sat down again, the cheerleaders went into their introduction cheer: "Johnny, Johnny, he's our man! If he can't do it, no one can! Johnny Silva!" And then, just because he could manage to throw an orange ball through a small metal hoop once in a while, the crowd went wild as scrawny, zitty Johnny Silva ran out from the locker room. We went through this same routine for each player, building up to the climax, which is when the cheerleaders would do a double cheer for the co-captains of the Buxton Eagles.

"This should be good," Russ said, checking the camera angle and repositioning it a bit. "These guys are so crazy."

They'd never seemed particularly crazy to me—just egomaniacal, like most of the high-school athletes at Buxton. But hey, now that I was friends with Russ, sort of, I was willing to give them the benefit of the doubt.

"Yeah," I said. "Can't wait to see what they're up to!"

"Ben and George, they're our men! If they can't do it, nobody can! Ben London and George Garrison!" The girls bounced even higher than usual, ricocheted off each other's hips, and split themselves in half, a maneuver that always made me cringe, especially when I was having my period. And despite the lack of a decent rhyme, wild enthusiasm greeted the heroic duo as they waltzed out into the gym. And I do mean *waltzed*.

George and Ben entered the gymnasium dancing arm in arm, or maybe I should say boob to boob, because each of them was wearing women's clothing, their chests sculpted so monumentally by whatever was stuffed underneath that their make-believe tits banged into each other. The crowd went nuts.

Then, still holding hands, they curtsied and ran up to join the cheerleaders. Ben was wearing a long blond wig and lots of jingly jewelry. George was in brown pigtails and a skirt that twirled wide to reveal some kind of lacy bloomers underneath. Both of them had slathered themselves with makeup, but they wore red Converse All Stars underneath their outfits, just so nobody misunderstood that they were still really basketball studs.

While the audience howled with laughter, the cheerleaders hoisted the two guys onto their shoulders, and they all did another cheer before Ben and George jumped off and made ridiculous attempts to do splits. I guess it was funny. I mean, yeah, they certainly looked silly with their hairy, muscled arms and legs sticking out from under the girly clothes and their padded boobs flopping all around. But everybody was laughing themselves sick, as if this role reversal was *so* unbelievable, it was killing them. I was confused. I hated to think I didn't have a good sense of humor, but I felt myself getting angry.

I guess it was supposed to be funny because being female was *so* much the opposite of who these big athletes were. But was that really true? I mean, this was hardly the first time I'd seen something like this. It seemed to me that the more macho the guy, the more he loved prancing around in high heels and a wig, just to prove to everybody that he could. He had enough testosterone to get away with it and not be ridiculed. But you had to wonder if there wasn't some part of these guys that was thrilled to wear the dress with the coconuts or whatever they were shoved inside. That they got off a little bit on the swingy hair brushing against their blushing cheeks. Maybe they needed a break from performing that whole machismo act day after day. Oh, I knew I'd never get any of them to admit it, but it seemed to me that the excitement of being a girl, if only for a few minutes, was about something more than just getting a good laugh from it.

The assembly was over a few minutes later, and everybody managed to pull themselves together enough to head back to class. I turned off the camera and unhooked it from the tripod, trying to look remarkably busy in case anybody felt like saying anything to me.

I could tell Russ was a little uncomfortable, but he tried to finesse it. "Man, I told you those two are crazy. They'll do anything."

"Yeah, that was *so crazy*," I said, not bothering to keep the sarcasm out of my voice.

He bent down to wind up the extension cords, but then turned back to me. "You didn't . . . I mean, you shouldn't take it the wrong way—"

"How is he *supposed* to take it? Is there a right way?"

Kita had run up the bleachers and was standing behind us, fuming. "That was the stupidest, most insensitive thing I've ever seen!"

Russ made a face at her. "Oh, come on, Kita. It was funny."

"*Funny?* You know they know about Grady—the whole gossipy school has been talking about nothing else all week. Don't they have a brain between them? This was offensive on about ten different levels."

I stared at Kita, trying to pretend I hadn't just tripped and fallen into the deep dark mine shaft of love from which escape is impossible. I finished breaking down the tripod and handed it to Russ, who had the electrical cords over his shoulder and the camera in his hand already.

"You're way off base, Kita," Russ said. "This isn't about that. It was just for laughs. You take things too seriously."

"I can't believe you're defending them, Russell!"

Russ was getting pissed off now too. "I'm not defending them! I don't even think they need defending!"

"Well then, you're as thickheaded as they are!"

Russ grunted. "I'm done listening to this, Kita—you're nuts. I'm going back to the TV studio. You can stand here and gripe to Grady if you want, but I don't see the problem. It was a *joke*." He hiked the equipment onto his shoulder and took off down the bleachers at an angry clip.

"Not a very funny one!" she called after him.

"Unfortunately, I think 99 percent of Buxton High would disagree with you there," I said.

"Buxton High," she said scornfully, "should get a clue. I'm sure it was meant to be offensive to you, but I think it's insulting to all women when guys parade around like that, acting like we're no more than jiggling body parts. I can assure you that George Garrison with sock boobs does not equal *me*!"

Then, almost before I knew it had happened, Kita put her arms around me in a fleeting hug. "And they don't equal you, either, Grady," she said. "You have more courage than a whole football team full of those idiots." Then she stomped down the bleachers and disappeared, taking my adoration with her.

Chapter Eleven

For the rest of the day I had the feeling people were staring at me even more than usual, as if they were trying to scope out my reaction. Sebastian, of course, met me at the door of the TV studio, ready to recap every thought he'd had since the morning's drag show.

"What kids are saying is that they don't think George and Ben's act had anything to do with you," he told me. "The party line is that it was just for laughs, guys have done this for years, what's the big deal, et cetera. But the fact that people are discussing it means it *is* a big deal. You've made them think about it. Well, not all of them, but at least the people who are capable of thinking."

"I'm thrilled," I said as I searched the unedited-video shelf for the footage we'd taken that morning.

"Russ has the videos," Sebastian said, pointing to the editing machine against the back wall where

Russ was already ensconced. Fine. He could edit this one all by himself. I could live without seeing George and Ben shaking their fake hooters again.

"You know what I've been thinking?" Sebastian asked.

"Not a clue."

His eyes got slitty, and I could tell this was going to be more than just a casual thought or momentary idea. No, the way Sebastian was spreading his hands before him in a descriptive swath promised a full-blown theory. "What if," he began, staring into the distance, "you put the most macho guy you could think of—say, Bruce Willis or somebody like that—on one end of a football field, and the most feminine woman you could think of—say Scarlett Johansson or . . . Beyoncé—on the other end . . ."

"You could sell a lot of tickets to that game."

He frowned at me. "What I'm saying is that if you had everybody else on earth lined up in between them according to how masculine or feminine they were, there would be a lot of people in the middle of the field, you know? Not everybody would be standing next to Bruce or Scarlett."

"Can I stand next to Beyoncé?"

"You know what I mean."

"This is a very big football field, Sebastian."

"I'm speaking metaphorically, Grady."

"And who gets to decide how masculine or feminine everybody is?"

"You decide for yourself."

"Most people would lie. They'd try to clump up around Bruce and Scarlett."

"Well then, some greater force would decide. The Great Scientist Who Knows Everything would decide."

Wouldn't that be perfect? Everybody exposed, turned inside out like me, on an enormous, metaphorical football field. I smiled and nodded. "I like it, Sebastian. Your brain is warped in a very interesting way."

"I know," he said, returning my smile.

SCENE:

The Feminine End of the Football Field

SCARLETT: Bee, you need to move over, hon. I'm supposed to be right here, at the very end.

BEYONCÉ: Well, that's not what I heard, sweetie. I'm at the end—you're second.

DANYA: [pushing her way to the goalpost] Get out of my way, you two. My father is a policeman!

SCARLETT: Who are you?

BEYONCÉ: You're not famous!

DANYA: Are you kidding? Everybody in Buxton knows who I am!

THE GREAT SCIENTIST WHO KNOWS EVERYTHING (no body; only a sweet, genderless voice): Danya, my dear, you don't belong at the end with Scarlett and Beyoncé.

DANYA: The hell I don't.

THE GREAT SCIENTIST WHO KNOWS EVERYTHING: See? With that mouth, I'm putting you down by Willis.

DANYA: [as she disappears into thin air] No-o-o-o-o!

SCARLETT: Wasn't she on *What Not to Wear*?

BEYONCÉ: [slipping past Scarlett and handcuffing herself to the goalpost] Entirely possible.

I pulled my hat tight around my head to walk home—it had gotten colder since yesterday, and the wind was whipping into my face. Mom probably would have picked me up if I'd called, and Sebastian would have happily followed me home again, but I really wanted to be alone for a while to think about all this stuff. Like, where would I be on the gender football field? Obviously not on the Beyoncé end, but not close to the Bruce Willis goal either. On the fifty-yard line? And if I was in the middle, what did that mean? That I was both male and female, or neither? Or something else altogether?

What made a person male or female, anyway? The way they looked? The way they acted? The way they thought? Their hormones? Their genitals? What if some of those attributes pointed in one direction and some in the other?

And some of this stuff had to do with the way you were raised, right? It's not as if we'd managed to stamp out stereotypes in this culture. In many places sugar and spice were still considered the opposite of snails and puppy-dog tails. When I decided I was a boy, I realized that if I wanted to pass, I'd have to learn to walk differently, talk differently, dress differently, basically act differently than I did as a girl. But why did we need to *act* at all? A quick look around Buxton High provided numerous cases of girls acting like girls and boys acting like boys—and very few people acting like themselves. Eve was a perfect example: She'd been a great girl until she hit Buxton, but now she was a high-pitched, low-self-esteem, capital-G Girl who couldn't relax and be Eve anymore.

So maybe it was silly for me to try to be somebody else's idea of a boy. I didn't need to swagger around and punch guys in the shoulder—that wasn't going to prove anything. There were still people who didn't succumb to the stereotypes. Sebastian certainly didn't punch or swagger, and he was a boy, although one who couldn't get a date to the Winter Carnival dance.

And why was changing your gender such a big honking deal anyway? People changed lots of other personal things all the time. They dyed their hair and dieted themselves to near death. They took steroids to build muscles and got breast implants and nose jobs so they'd resemble their favorite movie stars. They changed names and majors and jobs and husbands and wives. They changed religions and political parties. They moved across the country or the world—even changed nationalities. Why was gender the one sacred thing we weren't supposed to change? Who made that rule?

While I was marching along the sidewalk thinking about all this stuff, even though I was angry about a lot of it, I also felt pretty good, better than I had in a while. It was that hug from Kita that had done it. Just the fact that someone as fabulous as Kita Charles understood me and was on my side made me feel strong again. And Sebastian helped too, I had to admit. Maybe, eventually, everything would be okay again. There were still people who liked me, no matter what gender I claimed to be.

I was just about to open the kitchen door when Mom threw it open and came barreling out.

"Oh! I just left a note on the table for you and Laura," she said. "I'm going to the hospital. Gail called—Michael is sick."

"Really? He's so little," I said, following her to the car.

"I know. Gail's scared to death. He has a fever, and he's been vomiting all day."

"She's a nurse, though. Shouldn't she know what to do?"

"When it's your own child, you're too flustered. You can't think clearly." She climbed into the driver's seat.

"Can I . . . can I come with you?" I said. I wasn't sure why I wanted to go, but I did.

"Well, I guess," she said. "Here, you drive. I'm feeling pretty jumpy myself." She climbed back out of the car and tossed me the keys.

As I backed down the driveway, I noticed two red gift boxes lying on the lawn, obviously blown off the roof sled. I pointed them out to Mom.

"I wish the whole damn sled would blow down," she said. "I wish Rudolph would blow a fuse and his legs would break off at the knee."

"Mom!"

"Sorry. I'm not really in the Christmas spirit this year." She stared out her side window.

"How come Dad still puts this stuff up every year? I mean, we're all pretty sick of it. Couldn't you tell him . . ."

She sighed. "Apparently, I can't. Even when my poor mother was alive and horrified that her Jewish daughter was living in the Christmas House, even then I couldn't ask him to cut back on the extravagance, the decking of every possible hall with the biggest boughs available. He loves doing it so much—entertaining the whole town. Everybody but *us*."

I had the feeling that Dad's decorations were only a small part of Mom's current lack of cheer. It was mostly about me and the ripple effect I seemed to be having on everyone around me. Since I couldn't think of anything to say to make her feel better, we drove the rest of the way in silence.

As soon as we got to the hospital we saw Joanne, Gail's friend who's an ER nurse. She told us Michael had been admitted to the Newborn Pediatrics Unit and pointed us in the right direction.

"It's probably just a virus," Joanne said. "But they're going to keep him overnight and hydrate him. You can't be too careful with a baby."

When we got to the room, Gail was bent over a hospital bassinet in which Michael seemed to be whimpering himself to sleep. Lying in that big crib with an IV taped to his tiny hand, Michael appeared even smaller than I remembered. Gail looked up when we walked in, and tears started pouring down her face in what were obviously well-worn trails.

Mom gave her a hug, and then I did too because I couldn't think of anything to say.

"I can't believe this is happening," Gail said, her voice a wail. "After all the kids I've treated in this hospital, I still never imagined my own child in here."

"We saw Joanne downstairs," Mom said. "She said it looked like a virus. He's only staying overnight as a precaution."

Gail shook her head wildly. "You don't know. I've worked here for sixteen years. I can't tell you how often it *looks* like something simple, but then suddenly the fever spikes, or the white blood count drops, or—"

Mom put her arm around Gail and led her to the one comfortable chair in the room. "Sit down and take a deep breath, honey. You know too much for your own good. Most of the time, if it looks like a virus, it *is* a virus. You've said that to me a million times since my kids were born. When I was scared to death about a swollen throat or a weird rash, you'd tell me, 'Don't panic!'"

Gail looked up at Mom warily through the glaze of tears. "Yeah, but you usually panicked anyway."

"I know, but I was always the high-strung sister—you were the cool, calm one."

"That's because I never understood what it was like when the sick child was your own. I've never been this frightened, Judy. I feel like I'm losing my mind!"

Mom leaned down and held her hand. "I know."

Gail stared mournfully at the tiny body sleeping behind the bars. "I never understood before how overwhelming it is—the love a parent has for a child."

Mom nodded. "You can't explain it beforehand."

"If I lost Michael, I couldn't bear it. I think I would lose myself!"

"You aren't going to lose him," Mom told her sternly. "He's going to be fine." But when she straightened up again and turned to me, she was crying too.

"He's going to be okay, isn't he?" I whispered.

She nodded, brushing at her cheeks. "Yes, yes,

he will. Maybe you could find us some coffee somewhere, in a machine or at the cafeteria. That would be a big help."

"Sure, Mom."

"Get yourself something too. We might be here for a while." She dug some quarters out of her purse, and as she pressed the change and a few dollar bills into my hand, she squeezed it lightly, then leaned in to circle my back with her arms. "Thank you, honey. Thank you . . . Grady."

Chapter Twelve

Michael got out of the hospital the next day, and by the weekend he was fine again. Mom wasn't crying anymore or giving me spontaneous hugs, but she actually called me Grady two more times. The name didn't flow from her lips—it sort of stuck in her throat and she coughed it up—but I wasn't complaining.

Sebastian's mother picked us up after school on Friday, because we had to take the video camera home to tape the chorus concert that evening. As we were loading the stuff into her trunk, Sebastian asked her if I could stay for dinner.

"It'll be easier," he said, as if he needed an excuse. "We have to be back at the theater by six to get set up."

Mrs. Shipley was so tiny, she had to sit on a big pillow in order to see over the steering wheel. When she spoke, I was surprised to hear that her voice matched her stature.

"It's fine with me if Grady wants to stay for

dinner," she said, the teeny sound floating from her mouth like bubbles from a glass of champagne. "Of course, I don't cook, Grady," she said, turning her pointy chin in my direction. "Never bothered to learn how."

"I can make an omelet," Sebastian said. "Or grilled cheese sandwiches, if you'd rather."

"And salad, honey. You can make me a salad," she said as she peeked at the oncoming traffic and pulled out.

"Okay," Sebastian agreed.

When we got to Sebastian's house, an enormous place with more bookshelves than a bookstore and enough bedrooms for half a dozen kids, his mother curled herself into an easy chair in the living room, clicked on the gas fireplace with a remote control, and dove into a large book that had obviously been waiting for her return.

"That's all she ever does is read," Sebastian said as we poked through the refrigerator. "She's not much good at anything else, especially people."

"She seems nice, though," I said, thinking how every family is bizarre in its own way.

"Oh, she's nice," he said. "Kind of useless, but very nice."

"Did you tell her about me?"

"Sure."

"Really? And she's okay with it?"

"Why wouldn't she be?"

"Well, some mothers wouldn't be that happy to hear their son was hanging around with somebody like me."

He shrugged. "She checked some books out of the library about transgendered people and read up on the subject. Anything is okay by her as long as it's in a book. Besides, I'm sure she's amazed that *anybody* is hanging out with me."

It hadn't occurred to me that Sebastian didn't have friends—he certainly had a lot of acquaintances, and people seemed to like him. He was probably a little too odd, though, for anybody to want to hang with him all the time. Which made him the perfect friend for me, the complete oddball. Next to me Sebastian's idiosyncrasies seemed barely noticeable.

As promised, Sebastian had rented a DVD of *Napoleon Dynamite*, and we went into the den to watch it so we wouldn't bother his mother. At first I wasn't getting into it too much. The main character, Napoleon, was the epitome of dorkiness, wearing moon boots and badly fitting clothes, his curly hair surrounding his head like a matted fur hat. He mumbled and slumped and seemed barely able to keep his eyes open. He told completely unbelievable lies and carried Tater Tots out of the cafeteria in the cargo pocket of his pants.

But before long the bizarre humor of the film began to get to me. Napoleon was surrounded by people more wacko than he was, and the poor guy was just searching for the same things most teenage boys are: a best friend, a girlfriend, and a little respect. Before long I was hooting as loudly as Sebastian. When the film ended, we applauded.

"It's great, isn't it?" Sebastian asked. "I told you."

"Yeah, it's really funny and sort of heartbreaking at the same time."

Sebastian bounced on the couch. "That's another category of films I love: simultaneously funny and heartbreaking."

"You know what?" I said. "You're just like Napoleon."

Sebastian stopped bouncing and looked at me quizzically, obviously not sure how to take my comment.

"Ah . . . thanks, I guess. I don't dress *that* badly, do I?"

I laughed. "No, you don't look like him, although your nerd genes do sometimes show through your clever disguise."

"Admittedly."

"I mean, the way Napoleon just naturally takes up with the odd kids—the shy girl and then Pedro, the new kid with the mustache and the Spanish accent. He doesn't think about it—he just does it. And he kind of becomes their savior."

Sebastian looked a little embarrassed. "Maybe he just needed some friends."

"Still," I insisted, "most people wouldn't have chosen the oddballs for their friends."

"Well, they're crazy, then. The oddballs are always the most interesting people. Don't you think?"

I shrugged. "Who am I to disagree? I believe I've been crowned King of the Oddballs."

"King *and* Queen," he said as I followed him out to the kitchen. "How about if I just order us a pizza for dinner? That's what I do half the time anyway. It contains all the food groups, you know."

"Sounds like a plan to me," I said. "I don't want to discriminate against any food groups."

Sebastian called for pizza delivery, then got some vegetables from the fridge and began to cut up a red pepper and a few green onions.

"Your mother really doesn't ever cook?" I asked.

"Nope, never has. She's a very picky eater, too. She doesn't really *like* food much."

"So you make her a salad every night?"

"Not every night. Sometimes I make scrambled eggs and toast."

I paused a moment, then said, in my best imitation of the goofy drawl of Napoleon Dynamite, "Do the chickens have large talons?"

It was a line from the movie, and Sebastian got it immediately. He answered as the old Idaho farmer in the movie does: "I don't understand a word you just said."

We both grinned stupidly, as if this little exchange had been made in our own newly invented language. Which in a way was true.

Sebastian paid the pizza guy when he showed up, then delivered a pretty good-looking spinach salad to his mother in the chair by the fire.

"Did you start the coffee for me, sweetie?" she asked in her tinkly little voice.

"Just turned it on," he replied.

She thanked him without raising her eyes from the book. We took our pizza upstairs to Sebastian's room. Which was also huge, and also full of books.

"Have you actually read all these books?" I asked him.

"Not all of them, but lots of them. It's what we Shipleys do."

I nodded. "So, if I wasn't here, would you be eating with your mother?" I asked, trying to make some kind of sense out of this household.

"Well, I might eat in the same room with her, but she'd still be reading. And I probably would too."

"And if your dad was here, would he be reading too?"

"Oh, he's never here for dinner. Why come home for salad and take-out pizza? He eats in restaurants most of the time with his clients or his partners."

I thought of the usual Katz-McNair dinner-table routine—all three of us kids trying to broadcast our news louder than the others, Mom and Dad jumping up and down to get stuff we forgot to bring into the dining room and attempting to jam a few words of their own into the conversation. It was usually pandemonium, unless the whole thing was scripted, as on Christmas Eve.

"So," Sebastian said, "Russ Gallo and Kita Charles will probably be breaking up pretty soon. Then you can make your move."

I choked on a mushroom. "*What* are you talking about?"

He continued to calmly separate pepperoni rounds from mozzarella strings in order to eat the pepperoni first. "Anybody can see that Russ is not up to handling a woman like Kita. She's got places to go, things to do. She's not your run-of-the-mill Buxton High girl."

"No, she's not, but that has nothing to do with me. I don't know why you think I'm interested in K-Kita," I said, cheese tangling around my tongue like rope. Obviously, it didn't take a genius to see that I could barely even say the girl's name without falling apart. But Sebastian was kind enough to not point that out.

He chewed his slice carefully. "I'm just saying, the time may soon be approaching when you could make a move on Kita, if you were so inclined."

I had to laugh—the idea of me making a move on anybody at this point in my life was too ridiculous to contemplate.

"If Kita is as special and amazing as you say she is, why would she be interested in the school mutant?"

"Duh, Grady. That's exactly why she *would* be interested. You're both *special*. Didn't you learn anything from Mr. Rogers?"

Ridiculous. I was hardly special the way Kita was special. Nobody was. "Didn't you learn anything from Napoleon Dynamite?" I said. "Even he had the sense not to go after the best-looking girl in the school. Besides, Kita and Russ make a good couple—I don't see them splitting up."

"Wait and see. Russ is a nice guy," Sebastian said, "but he's just a regular guy. Nothing extra. You've got extra."

That I did. Extra in some places, and not quite enough in others. But would that make me interesting to the most amazing girl in Buxton?

I'd never been to a chorus concert before. Not surprisingly. The only people who showed up for this kind of activity were parents or maybe best friends. I was surprised—the singing was actually pretty good. And they all looked very professional: the girls in their white blouses and long black skirts, the five guys who'd had the courage to join the group in black tuxedos and bow ties. Of course, I couldn't help wondering—if I'd joined the chorus, what would I have been wearing? A long black skirt and a bow tie? Always the question.

It was nice to see everybody enjoying themselves up there, singing harmony and coming in at just the right places. I was stupidly happy that those five guys hadn't let their friends talk them out of joining a group that was obviously going to be 90 percent female. The guys sang as loud and strong as the girls.

Of course, my eyes were pretty much glued to Kita during the whole performance, so I couldn't really tell you who those five guys were. She had her hair pulled back with an elastic, but it still stood out gloriously around her face. What a beautiful face it was, her double ethnicities weaving themselves around each other in perfect harmony.

Russ Gallo was sitting in the back of the auditorium, not that far from where we had the camera set up. The place wasn't more than half full, and most people sat up close to the stage. Russ slumped in his chair and put his feet up on the seat in front of him; he didn't appear to be enjoying himself. Not that I spent much time looking at Russ, but when I did, he was studying his fingernails, not looking at the stage. I wondered if Kita could feel me staring at her. If she did, would she think the person who couldn't take his eyes off her was her boyfriend? If she realized it was me, Grady the *Special*, would it freak her out?

When the concert was over, Russ got up and ambled over to where Sebastian and I were packing up the equipment.

"Hey," he said, reaching down to pull in some wires.

"Hey," I said back, feeling immediately guilty for the betrayal of him that had been going on in my overactive brain.

"You guys want to come out and get something to eat with us?" he said.

"With you and Kita?" I asked.

"Sure."

Sebastian gave him an arched eyebrow look. "You guys want company?"

Russ shrugged. "Might be easier that way. Kita's still pissed off at me."

"About the Ben and George thing?"

"Yeah, that. And other stuff. I don't know. She's on my back all the time lately about one thing or another."

"Well, couples have their ups and downs," I said cheerily, as if I had any experience of couplehood or knew what the hell I was talking about.

"Yeah, I guess. Anyway, Kita will be happy to have you two along. She likes you."

I had a Sally Field moment: *She likes me, she really likes me!* But I came to my senses when I saw Kita walking down the aisle toward us, her jawbone arranged in a manner that seemed to be saying she didn't like anyone very much at the moment.

"The chorus sounded great," I said, trying to wipe the frown off her face. "I totally enjoyed it."

"Thanks, Grady," she said, shooting me a half-baked smile. "The harmony was off in the last song, though."

"Really?" Russ said. "I liked that one."

"You did, huh? What *was* the last song?" Kita turned on Russ and stared him deep in the eyes. I could imagine crumbling to dust under that stare.

"You know, the one about . . . wasn't it about a . . . a train or something?" Russ looked to us for help, but it was too late.

"Tell him, Grady. What was the last song we sang?"

My betrayal fantasy was coming true. "It was 'Swing Low, Sweet Chariot,'" I said quietly, thanking God I was a better listener than Russ.

"That's right. There aren't any trains in it, Russ. There's a chariot in it, but no trains." Kita propped one arm on her hip and pursed her lips, glaring at him.

"Oh, I guess I was thinking of a different song . . ."

"Admit it, Russell. You weren't even listening. You didn't want to come, so you just sat out here pouting. I could see you. You decided before you showed up that you wouldn't like it, so you didn't."

Russ turned his palms up and appealed to Sebastian and me to help him. "Can you believe this? I told you, Kita, I'm not that into singing. I *came*, didn't I? What do you want from me?"

She shook her head. "I want you to act like you give a damn about me, but that obviously isn't going to happen, is it?"

I was embarrassed for Russ that he was being insulted in front of two schlubs like us. He had to get mad; what else could the guy do?

"Look, Kita, I've tried to be whatever it is you expect a boyfriend to be, but I'm obviously not perfect enough for you. Maybe you should find somebody who is."

"Or maybe just somebody who's more emotionally mature than a twelve-year-old!" Kita shot back.

"That's it!" Russ yelled. "I'm sick of you ragging on me all the time! So I'm not perfect. Boohoo. Neither are you, Kita! *Neither are you!*"

Sebastian and I broke down the equipment, pretending we were invisible. In another minute, Russ was headed out of the auditorium, barking a few last nasty words back at Kita. Once he was gone, the fight went out of her and she slumped down onto the arm of a chair.

"Did you and Russ just break up?" Sebastian

asked her, managing not to sound too pleased about it.

"Is that what it looked like?" Kita asked.

"Did to me."

"Well, I guess we did, then." She didn't seem 100 percent happy about the idea.

"I'm sorry," I said. And then, lamely, repeated myself. "I'm really sorry."

"It's not your fault," she said.

"I know, but . . ." But what?

Sebastian was hard at work, not just packing up the video stuff, but also plotting the course of my life. "What you guys really ought to do is go out and get some coffee or something. Kita needs somebody to talk to."

I looked at him in panic. "Your mother is picking us up any minute, isn't she?"

"Well, she's picking *me* up, and I can take all the equipment. But you live close enough to walk home, don't you?" His eyebrow was trying to send me a signal of some sort, leaping around the left side of his forehead.

"Would you mind, Grady?" Kita said, looking up at me sadly. "I don't really want to go home alone right now. My mother could pick us up later and drop you off at your house."

"Well, I guess I could, but"—I turned to

Sebastian once more—"maybe we could all go, and Kita's mother could drop you off . . ."

Sebastian shook his head sorrowfully. "I wish I could, but I have a trig test tomorrow, and I've barely studied. I have to get home."

Right. Did Sebastian even take trigonometry? My hands were so sweaty, I could barely hold onto the camera case. We all carried the equipment outside and stacked it in the back of Mrs. Shipley's waiting Volvo. She and Sebastian both waved their little hands at us as they drove away, leaving me alone with Kita Charles.

It was only two blocks to the August Moon diner, but they were the longest two blocks I'd ever walked. Kita was dragging her feet a little, and I kept walking too fast and getting ahead of her, then realizing it and dropping back. But walking right next to her, banging elbows, made me kind of light-headed, so then I'd speed up again and leave her behind. If anyone had been watching, they would have thought my cruise control was broken.

Finally, we slumped into a booth at the diner.

"I'm sorry, Grady," Kita finally said. "I shouldn't have made you come with me. You probably just want to go home."

"No, I don't!" I assured her. "If you want to

talk or anything, I'm here. I mean, I'm glad to be here. I mean, I'm not glad you broke up, but . . ."

She sighed. "I shouldn't have been so mean to Russ. He's a nice guy, and he tries to do the right thing, but somehow we just don't work together. We're too different—we get on each other's nerves."

I couldn't imagine Kita ever getting on my nerves. We ordered coffee and fries, then sat in silence until the coffee arrived.

"You must think I'm terrible, don't you? A spoiled brat," Kita said.

"No, I don't! I've always thought you were really . . . really nice." I'd almost said "wonderful," but at the last minute I managed to switch to the most benign compliment possible.

"I used to think I was a nice person, but lately . . ." A tear rolled down her cheek. *Lord, save me.*

The waiter plopped the basket of fries and a small bowl of ketchup in between us, unaware of the drama taking place before him. I handed Kita my napkin, even though she had one in front of her too. "You *are* a nice person, Kita. You're a great person. You're probably my favorite person in the whole school!" *Whoa, back up. Too much information.* "I mean, you know, except for, like, Sebastian." *Shut up! Shut up!*

"Thanks, Grady," she said, smiling a little. "I like you too. Are you and Sebastian a couple or something?"

"What?" I could feel the heat spreading across my face and imagined the scarlet color that came with it.

"I wasn't sure if . . . you know . . . if you were into guys or girls now."

I reached for the coffee cup to disguise my embarrassment. "Well, no. I like girls. I always have liked girls, only now I like them as a boy, I guess."

She nodded. "That's good."

"It is?"

"Sure. Now you're a boy who likes girls *and* understands them. How many of those are there? In my experience, not many." She looked into my eyes and grinned as she toyed with a long french fry, flopping it around in the ketchup before finally bringing it to her mouth and chopping it in half.

"Well, I don't know if . . . some people wouldn't . . . I mean, not everyone thinks . . ." I had no idea what I was even trying to say. She had me hypnotized, my eyes following the dancing potato.

"I like you, Grady," she said, clearly, so there could be no mistaking it. She took the uneaten half of her french fry and held it in front of my mouth. "Let's share."

I opened my mouth and let her put the fry inside it. I wasn't at all sure I'd be able to chew and breathe at the same time with her looking at me like that. But somehow I managed to live through the most astounding moment of my life so far.

Chapter Thirteen

Sebastian called two minutes after I got home. I hadn't even had a chance to answer my mother's questions about why the filming went so late.

"Who gave you a ride home?" she asked as she handed me the kitchen phone—the old kind that was still tethered to the wall—then stood there, watching me.

"I'll tell you in a minute," I said, but she didn't move.

Since the main living areas were still on display, Dad and Charlie were in the kitchen too, staring at a basketball game on the small TV on the counter. Laura was spending the night at her friend Mira's house, so at least she wasn't there to spy on me.

"So what happened?" Sebastian screamed at me. "Where did you go? What did she say?"

"I can't talk right now, Sebastian. I just got home, and—"

"What do you mean, you can't talk? This would never have happened if I hadn't set it up! I had your back, just like Napoleon and Pedro! You owe me details!"

"I know, I know," I said, then let my mind drift.

KITA: [brandishes a golden fried potato] I like you, Grady. Let's share.

GRADY: [tongues the french fry, nibbling it out of her fingers] Whatever you say.

KITA: I say, the hell with Russell Gallo. You're the one I've been waiting for all my life. You're my twin, my perfect match.

GRADY: And you're mine, Kita.

KITA: Feed me, Grady. Feed me. [opens her mouth]

[GRADY picks up another fry, dips it in ketchup, and twirls it into Kita's chin, spewing ketchup across her face and blouse.]

KITA: [wiping red goo off herself] Grady! Look what you did! You ruined everything!

[GRADY crawls under the table and curls into a fetal position.]

Jeez, even my imagination couldn't come up with a decent outcome for me and Kita. The actual evening hadn't been *that* bad.

The phone in my hand was chirping. "Grady! Tell me!"

My mom had finally left my side and was folding laundry on the kitchen table; I turned away from her. "We shared a french fry," I whispered.

"A what? A french fry? Is that code or something?"

"Look, why don't you come over tomorrow? We'll talk about it then."

He sighed. "You have *got* to get a cell phone. What time should I come?"

"Say, eleven. I want to sleep in."

"Fine. I'll be up at dawn, waiting."

"Don't expect much, Sebastian. It was really just a french fry."

I hung up and turned around to find my mother staring at me. "What was 'just a french fry'?" She obviously thought I was speaking a secret language too.

I sighed. If only there were something to tell. "It's nothing. I went to get something to eat with this girl I know. Kita Charles. She just broke up with her boyfriend, and she needed somebody to talk to."

"I never heard you mention her before. Did you just meet her?"

"Yeah, sort of. I know her boyfriend. Her ex-boyfriend."

"Uh-huh." She examined me quizzically. "I went to the window when I heard the car in the driveway. It looked like there was an Asian woman driving."

"That's Kita's mother. She's Japanese American."

"So, Kita is Japanese?"

"Partly. And partly African American."

"Really? Well, I imagine she does need friends—I'm glad you're helping her. I keep reading about how difficult it is for those kids."

"What kids?"

"Kids who are half in one culture and half in another. It's hard for them to know which one to identify with."

"Kita has lots of friends," I said. "Of all kinds. She doesn't even need me. I just happened to be around when she broke up with her boyfriend."

She smiled at me. "You're a good . . . kid." What a laugh. She thought I was doing Kita a favor or something. She had it all backward.

The game must have finished up: Dad turned off the TV. "So, what did they have to say about the decorations when they dropped you off?" he asked. Even after all these years, he liked to hear what everybody thought of his efforts.

"Well, Kita said 'wow' about fifteen times. Her mother seemed a little bit confused by it all."

"Tell 'em to come by on Christmas Eve for the big show!" he said, undaunted. "Which reminds me, tomorrow is costume-fitting day, in case any seams or hems need to be let out or anything. So your mom has time to fix things."

Charlie stopped on his way to the stairs. "I don't want to do that Tiny Tim thing this year, with the crutch and everything. I'm too big."

That was certainly true. Even last year Dad could barely carry him on his shoulders, and Charlie hadn't gotten any smaller with another year's worth of sitting on the couch inhaling Cheez Doodles.

And it's not as if we really put on *A Christmas Carol* anyway—that would be way too much, even for Dad. We dressed like Dickens's characters, and we ate turkey and pudding—chocolate pudding, not plum pudding made with suet and brandy like in the original. But the rest of the show was mostly in mime. We were miked to the outside, but the scripted lines were few and mostly belonged to Dad, which was fine with the rest of us. It's true that ending the show with Charlie on a chair shouting, "God bless us, every one!" always got a big cheer from the crowd, but maybe that was just because the whole thing was over and the parents could finally get their kids to go to Grandma's house for *their* dinner.

Dad, of course, looked crushed. "But how will we end the show without Tiny Tim?"

"I'll still *say* it, if you want, but I feel stupid limping around with that crutch and pretending to be a baby."

"But it's a *show*, Charlie!" Dad begged.

"Look, Joe," Mom said. "We're all getting a little bit tired of doing this every year. You can't expect the children to be as excited about it as they used to be when they were younger."

"Why not?" He really didn't know. Mom and Charlie and I looked at each other, none of us able to say what needed to be said.

"It's late," Mom finally said. "We'll talk about it tomorrow."

Charlie and I tore up the stairs so we didn't have to see that sad, confused look on Dad's face another second.

At a quarter to eleven the next morning, Sebastian's mother's car pulled into the driveway. I opened the door with a piece of bacon in my hand.

"Ooh, can I have that?" Sebastian said, taking it from my fingers. "Haven't had bacon in ages. Oh, and my mother wants to know when to pick me up. Am I staying all day?"

"Sure. I can drive you home later."

He ran back to give his mother the message. She was swaddled in a fur coat that made her head look even smaller than it really was. She stuck her head out the window and yelled to me, "I think one of your teddy bears has fallen over!"

"Thanks!" I said. "I'll put it back up later."

"I'll do it!" Sebastian said, and ran right over to set Pooh in an upright position again. His mother backed out, smiling and waving. She did seem quite pleased by our friendship. And I had to admit that I was too. Sebastian wasn't Eve—he could never replace the friend I'd had since I was a little kid—but he'd proved himself to be on my side when I needed a friend, which was a lot more than I could say for Eve, or anyone else for that matter. Except Kita.

Sebastian was happy to sit at the kitchen table and eat a few more pieces of bacon while I finished the eggs Mom had made for me. He seemed fascinated by my rowdy family—Mom and Charlie arguing, again, about why he couldn't have a dog for Christmas, Dad spouting lines of dialogue from the Christmas script to remind himself when to say what ("Sit you down before the fire, my dear . . .") and Laura, running in the back door and then shrieking from upstairs half a minute after getting a phone call from some mystery male.

Still yelling, Laura came pounding down the stairs like a much larger person. "Mom! Mom! He asked me to the dance! I'm going to the dance!"

"So, that was Jason, I guess," Mom said. She was obviously on the inside regarding Laura's current hopes and dreams.

"It was Jason!" Laura said, twirling in a circle. "I'm going to the dance!"

"Who's Jason? What dance?" I wanted to know.

She gave me the *Duh* look. "The Winter Carnival dance. And Jason Kramer is *the* most popular boy in our entire class. And *I'm* going with him!"

"That's great," Sebastian said, grinning. "Grady and I are going too, you know."

The color drained out of Laura's face. "What?"

I knew what she was thinking. "He doesn't mean we're going together. I mean, we *are*, but only to videotape it for the cable channel."

She still wasn't looking too good. "You mean, you're going to be running around shoving a camera in people's faces all night?"

"We don't interrupt anything," Sebastian

explained. "We just stand on the sidelines and tape whatever's going on. People hardly know we're there."

Laura didn't look convinced of our invisibility. "*I'll* know you're there. And you better not take any pictures of me!"

I held up a hand like a traffic cop. "Whatever."

"So, I suppose you want to get a new dress?" Mom said.

"Please, Mom? I don't have anything nice enough."

That might not have been true, but Mom agreed to buy her a dress anyway. She seemed almost as excited about it as Laura. I guess Mom figured it was about time somebody acted like a real girl around here.

"She gets a *dress* and I can't even have a *pet*?" Charlie said indignantly. "That is just no fair!"

Dad interrupted the potential argument. "Enough with the dog, Charlie. Time to try on costumes. I didn't bring the hoop skirts down from the attic yet, but these are the rest of the girls' clothes." He opened a big box and started pulling out bonnets and aprons and long flowery dresses.

"Laura, this is yours," he said, handing her a long blue plaid skirt with a matching shawl and white blouse. "Judy, your red taffeta."

As Mom reluctantly took her dress and Dad reached back into the box, I think we all realized the problem at the same moment. He pulled out the green flowered dress I'd worn for the last few years, the one with lace at the cuffs and a ruffled apron.

Why didn't I think of this before now? There was no way on earth I was flouncing around in that dress again, or any dress, in front of half the town. I'd never liked that flowery thing anyway. It was too fancy for me—too feminine. It had been Mom's dress first, but as I got taller, she gave it to me and made herself a dressier one, which Dad thought she ought to have.

Dad pulled the dress out of the box, and we all stood there, looking at it.

"Oh," he said, finally. "I guess . . . Angela wore this." He said it sadly, as if Angela had died. Which was the way it seemed as we all stood there staring at the green dress that Angela would never wear again. For a minute even *I* missed Angela, the girl with the unruly curls who helped Mrs. Cratchit—or whoever Mom was supposed to be—get the turkey on the table. The good girl who had morphed into the bad boy. *Grady, you ruin everything*.

"Well," Dad said, cramming the dress back

into the box, "let's open the boys' box. There's probably something in there Grady could wear."

"You must have an extra pair of pants, Joe," Mom said. "I can take them in and hem them."

"Doesn't he need a frock coat too?" Laura wanted to know.

"He can get by with a vest. We're inside, after all," Mom said.

"I only wear a vest," Charlie said.

And just like that, it was over, with nobody freaking out at all. I let out the breath I'd been holding since the first green flower peeked over the edge of the box. Stunned by my entire family's miraculous composure, I went into the bathroom to try on a pair of Dad's pants. They were quite a bit too big, but Mom pinned them in twenty-two places and promised she'd make them fit well enough.

It turned out I could wear Charlie's old vest, but he'd need new clothes to fit over his expanded chest and stomach.

"See, I told you. I'm way too big to be Tiny Tim this year. Can't we just skip that part?" Charlie begged.

"Or you could just skip the junk food for a while," Mom suggested.

"I'm not going to get skinny by next week no matter what I eat," Charlie said.

Sebastian cleared his throat. "Um, if you really need a Tiny Tim, maybe *I* could do it."

We all looked at him—he was certainly the correct size. "You *want* to be Tiny Tim?" I asked him.

"Sure. I mean, people call me that anyway. And I've always wanted to act."

"There's not much acting involved," Charlie told him. "Mostly you ride on Dad's shoulders, hobble around on a crutch, and then deliver your one line."

"That would be great!" Dad said happily, pounding Sebastian on the back. "That's what we need around here, some new blood, somebody with some enthusiasm."

Laura and Charlie and I exchanged looks. *Great.* Now Dad would expect us all to get infected with Sebastian's "enthusiasm."

"In fact," Dad continued, "I was thinking we need a new script this year. We don't have any little kids anymore—you could all memorize more lines. I was thinking I might take a look at the original *Christmas Carol* and do a longer adaptation of it, something we could really sink our teeth into!"

No, no. This was bad.

"Oh, Joe, it's awfully late to start a big project

like that," Mom said, trying to mask a look of terror. "I mean, it takes time to memorize something new. Why don't we just stick to what we know—"

"I'll write one!" I said, the words forming already in my head. "We won't have to memorize it. I'll give everybody a script that night. It'll be fun."

Heads swiveled toward me in shock. "*You're* going to write it?" Laura asked.

"I didn't know you were interested in playwriting," Dad said.

"Oh, yeah," Sebastian said. "Grady is quite a scriptwriter!" His eyes were sparkling, and I knew he thought it was going to be a joint project. We'd see. I had a plan in mind already.

"Well, okay," Dad said. "That's terrific. I'm glad our seasonal shenanigans have inspired you."

Oh, they certainly had. I could hardly wait to get started.

Sebastian was duly impressed with my room. "Jeez, don't your parents ever make you throw stuff away?"

I guess I hadn't realized I was as big a pack rat as my Dad. "Sebastian, my parents never *let* me throw anything away. You never know what might be useful someday."

He'd begun to burrow through the box of old birthday cards on my desk when he suddenly remembered his mission.

"Wait, you still haven't told me about Kita. What happened? All you said was something about sharing a french fry."

"Yeah, that was the high point."

"A french fry was the high point?"

I nodded. "She ate half and fed me the other half."

Sebastian's eyes got huge. "That's amazing. You ate it from her *hand*?"

"Yup."

"So, *then* what?"

"So, then she started talking about Russ, and why she liked him so much, and why he annoyed her so much, and why she wanted to break up with him, and why she knew she would miss him terribly. Russ, Russ, Russ, for half an hour."

Sebastian digested the information. "That's not so good."

"No, it wasn't."

"Did you give her any advice?"

"Me? What do I know about breaking up with somebody? Plus, I don't want to give her advice—that's what a girlfriend gives you. I don't want to be her girlfriend."

"You should have fed *her* a french fry," he suggested.

I shook my head. "It had already been done."

"So, you just sat there and listened?"

"And ate the rest of the fries."

"Man, that's a sad story."

"You're telling me."

He sighed and then perked up again. "Well, next time you'll be more prepared. And by then she'll be over Russ, too. This was just the first step."

Was he kidding? "Sebastian, she's never going out with me again. It was a fluke, a one-time event, not a first step."

"You never know," he said, smiling. "I might have another idea."

Chapter Fourteen

Sebastian and I worked on the new script all afternoon. I had to fill him in on what Dad's original scene had been like—he hadn't actually watched it since he was a kid. Like I said, there wasn't much dialogue in the original. We mostly mimed our great joy as Dad Cratchit stumbled though the door with Tiny Tim/Chubby Charlie on his shoulders. I guess we were the Cratchits after Scrooge had seen all the ghosts and been frightened into kindness; Bob Cratchit received a living wage now and we could enjoy the season these days. In fact, I'm sure Dickens's impoverished characters never dreamed of having this much junk decorating their parlor.

We would start with Dad and Charlie taking off their hats and mufflers, and then we'd all sit around the Christmas tree while Dad got the fire going. Laura would hand out a wrapped gift to each of us, and we'd open them one at a time—the same presents every year. Dad got a pipe, which he pretended to light and smoke, drawing in a deep breath of apparently delightful pollution. Mom opened a box to reveal a new bonnet, which she modeled for the crowd before laying it lovingly back in its tissue paper for another year. Laura and I both got gloves, which we pretended were our hearts' desire, pulling them on immediately and playing a little clapping game. And Tiny Charlie always got two gifts, because, of course, he was beloved *and* sick: a pair of socks and a bag of candy. I thought it was funny that Dad's script called for Charlie to share his candy with the rest of us; obviously that's what selfless little Tim would have done, but Chunky Charlie would have scarfed the entire bag down by himself and screamed if anybody else came close to it.

There were a few extra gifts, because sometimes Aunt Gail joined us, and Eve had been a regular participant the past few years too. Gail always got an embroidery hoop and some colorful thread, while Eve rejoiced over an old math textbook that she pretended was *Romeo and Juliet*. You couldn't tell from outside what the book really was anyway. It was upsetting to remember how much Eve had enjoyed those Christmas spectacles. More than we ever did, I'm sure. Her own father was usually overworked and grumpy; he regularly lectured everyone in sight about how Christmas was merely a ploy to make retailers rich and him poor. Under normal circumstances Eve thought our dad was a prince; at Christmastime she thought he was a god for his devotion to the kinds of rituals that could never occur at her house.

After the gift opening Mom and Dad had a few lines to say about the joys of being surrounded by one's family, and how we'd put aside our worldly worries to rejoice in the season. Then we'd all trek happily into the dining room (except Charlie, who limped in), miming great hunger even though five thirty was an hour earlier than our usual dinner. Laura and I would disappear into the kitchen and bring out steaming dishes (from the microwave) of mashed potatoes, green beans, and biscuits. Finally, Mom would come from the kitchen, holding a platter before her on which an enormous turkey stood in for the goose of the Dickens story. Dad always ran to help her set the heavy plate in the middle of the table, and they exchanged a few lines about how this was surely the finest goose ever we'd had.

We'd take our seats around the table and join hands. Dad's baritone would burst into a prayer of thanks, for the season, for the glorious food laid before him, and for the gathering of his most beloved around him. I have to admit, I sometimes got a little chill during this part. Oh, I was embarrassed by it too—what teenager wouldn't be? But Dad meant it; he wasn't acting. Or, he was acting, but he meant it too. He loved doing this, declaring his devotion to us, and his passion for Christmas, in front of half the town.

By this time it was almost over. I'd get up and wander over to the drapery pull while Dad took up a carving knife and dug into the turkey. Laura and the guests held up their plates for the first slice, and Charlie stood up on his chair, holding onto the back to support his gimpy leg. He had his little cane in his hand and would raise it high over his head and declare, "God bless us, every one!" I'd count to ten so we could appreciate the applause from outside for a minute; then I'd slowly pull the curtains closed. Dad would turn off the inside microphones and get the plastic carolers warbling again. And then we could all eat dinner in peace.

The whole thing took less than twenty minutes, usually, but somehow it had become the most important event of our season, overshadowing everything else. When we were little kids, it was fun to show off for the neighborhood, but the older we got, the more ridiculous it all seemed, and the more humiliating. I guess Mom always disliked it. But whatever our feelings, the event defined our year, measuring how much we'd grown by both the number of inches our hems had to be let out and by our ability to understand the drama and enact our roles.

This year the roles themselves would grow. They would more perfectly fit their actors, who would, with any luck, be bidding their final farewell to the entire enterprise.

I did most of the writing myself, but Sebastian was surprisingly good with dialogue too. Several times we had to back up and tone things down a bit so Dad wouldn't end up looking like a fool in front of the neighbors.

"Is this too much?" Sebastian would ask.

"Maybe," I'd answer.

"You know, your dad isn't going to be happy about this."

"Can you think of a better way to get him to stop torturing us?"

"Maybe you could just ask him."

I shook my head. "My mother is Jewish and she's been doing this for ten years already. We're all too gutless."

When we got to the ending, though, Sebastian stood firm. "You cannot take out the last line. Your dad said I could be Tiny Tim, and I want to say that line!"

"Why?"

"*Why?* Are you kidding me? It's a famous line! I want to stand on a chair and say it. When will I ever have a chance like this again?"

"I didn't know you were a frustrated actor," I said.

"I didn't either, but maybe I am."

So we worked the ending around to conclude with Tiny Sebastian, balancing on his chair, demanding blessings for everyone. Dad would be glad we'd kept the finale too.

We'd just finished a decent first draft when Mom called upstairs. "Phone for you . . . Grady."

I answered with my usual doubt. "For me?"

"It's Kita!" Sebastian said. "I bet she's calling you to ask you out again!"

"Don't be ridiculous," I said. But as I headed to Mom and Dad's room to get the phone, my heart began to thump. What if it *was* Kita? Who else would be calling me? Was it possible?

"Hello?" I croaked, my voice suddenly hoarse.

Sebastian stood so close to me I could hear him breathe. *Who is it?* he mouthed.

I turned away from him and tried to concentrate on the voice on the phone.

"It's me," the voice said. "Please don't hang up!"

Eve. Damn.

"I told you, we aren't friends anymore. You have to stop calling me."

"I know, but I have something important to tell you. Please—"

Sebastian was making all kinds of faces to get my attention and I finally just said, "It's Eve," to get him to back down.

"Is somebody there with you?" Eve wanted to know.

"Yes. Surprisingly, not everyone thinks I have a contagious affliction."

"I don't think that!" Eve said. "Who's there?"

"Sebastian Shipley."

"Oh yeah, you were with him the other day too."

"Yes, Judas, I was."

"Angela, I'm sorry—"

"Angela doesn't live here anymore," I said.

She sighed. "I know. I mean Grady. I really miss you, whatever your name is." I could hear the tightness in her throat. If she started to cry, I'd be tempted to be nice to her, which I was not in the least ready to do.

"Look, Eve, I have to go. I'm busy—"

"No! Don't hang up! I have to tell you something! Please!"

I was afraid to listen to her. What if I got all

confused about whether I hated her or not? It felt good to hate her at the moment. I needed to hate her.

"I can't, Eve. I can't talk to you right now."

"Then, then . . . let me talk to Sebastian! Can I talk to him?"

That surprised me. "What do you want to talk to him for?"

Sebastian's ears pricked up and he started pointing to himself. *Me? She wants to talk to me?*

"Just for a minute, Grady, please."

Her use of my new name softened me. I sighed and handed the phone over to Sebastian, who grabbed it excitedly.

"Hello?" he said. There was a silly grin on his face, and I wondered if he'd ever actually talked to a girl on the phone before.

After a few pleasantries, Sebastian got quiet. Eve was obviously telling him something complicated. Every now and then he'd nod and say "uh-huh" or "whoa." His face began to tighten into a scowl. I couldn't imagine what Eve's news might be.

Finally he nodded gravely and said, "Don't worry, Eve, we'll figure out something. And we won't say who told us either. Okay. Thanks for calling. Bye." He handed the phone back to me and I hung it up.

"So?" I asked.

"I think you might owe her for this one," he said.

"Are you kidding? She's been rotten to me ever since—"

"Yeah, but this is pretty big," he said. I followed him back into my room and he shut the door.

"Danya has a trick planned. An ingeniously sick plan, as you might imagine."

"A trick on me?"

He nodded. "She figured out that you use Ms. Unger's office shower after gym class. She has a study hall that hour, which is easy to get out of, so on Monday she's planning to go there with her cronies and steal your regular clothes *and* your gym clothes while you're showering."

"What? That . . . that . . ." I was having trouble coming up with a name bad enough for her. What would I do if I came out of the shower and all my clothes were missing?

"That's not all of it. She's going to leave other clothes for you to wear instead, apparently some very sexy, revealing outfit of hers and a pair of high heels. Which she figures you'll have to wear or go naked."

There was a banging in my chest that felt more

like a wrecking ball than a heart. "Are you kidding me? What . . . I can't believe it!" Except, unfortunately, I could. I could totally imagine walking out of the shower room wearing Danya's slutty clothes, and just how horrible I'd feel, and what people would say, and how they'd look at me. How they'd laugh. And I was perfectly able to imagine the grin on Danya's face. It nauseated me.

"Yeah," Sebastian agreed. "Thank God Eve had the nerve to tell you."

"The nerve? She has a nerve all right. She was probably in on the whole thing from the beginning." I sank down on the bed while Sebastian paced.

After a minute, he pulled a roll of mints from his pocket and offered me one. "You do realize that Eve is terrified of Danya, don't you? I mean, this is the kind of thing Danya does to people who get on her bad side. Eve is taking a big chance even telling you about it."

I crushed my mint into dust. "Then why is she doing it? Eve has always been afraid of her shadow. What if her telling me is part of the trick? I don't trust her."

"I believe her," Sebastian said.

"Why? Did she start crying? That doesn't mean anything—she cries about everything."

"No, I mean, I believe she really still wants to

be your friend. I believe she feels terrible about what's happened. She's not a bad person, Grady—she just didn't know enough to steer clear of Danya and she got caught in her trap."

Suddenly *I* felt like crying. Was I going to have to worry about every single thing I did now? Even something as simple as showering after gym class? Why couldn't people just leave me alone? Who was I hurting, anyway? Why did I have to defend my right to be the person I was? I let my head sink down into my hands—it suddenly felt too heavy for my neck to support on its own.

Sebastian sat down next to me. "I know, it sucks," he said.

I nodded.

"We'll get her back," he said.

"How?"

"I don't know yet, but I'll think of something."

Which was good to know, but not immediately helpful. There were people who wanted to hurt me, to humiliate me, and maybe there always would be. I felt like crawling under a rock and staying there for the next few years.

"We need to take a walk," Sebastian said finally. He put a hand on my back. "I know. Let's go to the pharmacy and visit Wilma."

*

"Hey, there!" Wilma called. "You boys back for more peppermint shampoo?"

You boys. She said it so naturally.

Sebastian nodded. "It's great stuff."

"Oh, it really is," Wilma said. "I got myself a bottle of it on your recommendation, and you were right. It smells good *and* it tingles. I was hoping you'd come back in so I could tell you." She grinned widely.

"My friend, Grady, is getting some today too," Sebastian said, handing me a bottle from the shelf.

I was? I stared at him, but I took the shampoo.

"Oh, you'll love it!" Wilma said. As she rang up the sales, she continued talking. "You boys go to the high school?" *Boys*.

"We do," Sebastian said.

"I got a niece goes there—a freshman. She says there's a big dance coming up. She's all excited about it. You two going to that?"

I cleared my throat to risk a few words. "We're actually going to be filming it for the cable TV channel." It was hard to gauge how masculine your own voice might sound.

But Wilma didn't flinch. "You *are*? It'll be on TV?"

"Not until after the holidays," I told her. "We'll have to edit it first."

"Well, my goodness. Katy'll be thrilled about that! If you see a tall girl with brown curly hair wearing a blue dress, you make sure to take lots of pictures of her, okay?"

"We sure will," Sebastian assured her as we took our bags and headed for the door.

"Bye, boys. See you later!"

Yes, she would. In fact, I might become a Wilma groupie. As long as she kept calling me "boy." Maybe I should ask Wilma to the Winter Carnival.

WILMA: Oh, look, there's my niece. [waves] Hi, Katy!

GRADY: I must say, Wilma, without your name tag and red smock, you look just like a freshman yourself.

WILMA: Aren't you a doll to say so, Grady.

GRADY: [leading her to the dance floor] Shall we boogie down, Wilma?

WILMA: [snuggling up] Sure! Ooh, Grady, you reek of peppermint.

GRADY: [copping a feel] I think that's you, my dear.

WILMA: [laughing] I think we're the stinkiest couple here!

GRADY: I hope so, Wilma. I hope so.

"So," Sebastian said as he walked along, swinging

his shampoo, "I think I've got a plan."

"A plan? Oh, yeah." I'd almost forgotten about my forthcoming humiliation. Not everybody liked the boy as much as Wilma did.

"Ms. Unger is on your side, right? She lets you use her shower and bathroom."

"Yeah. She's not exactly my buddy, though."

"Maybe not, but I'm betting she doesn't care much for Danya."

"Probably a safe bet."

"Right. And that will work to our advantage." Sebastian said. "Let's go back to your house and place a call to the girls' gym teacher."

Chapter Fifteen

Ms. Unger was crazy about the idea. It helped that she disliked Danya as much as I did. Her exact words were, "I've been wanting to trim that girl's sails since she first walked into my class."

So on Monday, after the usual ball-bouncing in the gym, Ms. Unger told us to run three laps and then head for the showers—she had to go down to the principal's office for a minute. I knew most kids wouldn't do the whole three laps, but we'd still have enough time. I ran the laps, then slipped into Ms. Unger's office quietly, as I'd been doing for several weeks. Some of the other girls had obviously heard about Danya's plot—they giggled nervously as I walked by, but I ignored them. I didn't close the outer office door all the way, just enough so that no one could watch me going into the bathroom instead of the shower room. As soon as I was inside, I knocked on the wall that separated the two spaces. The shower came on immediately.

When I'd gotten changed before gym, I'd left

my school clothes and a second set of gym clothes outside Ms. Unger's shower, all in a heap as if I'd just dropped them there. As I put on the other clothes I'd stashed in the bathroom, I listened at the door. Danya was stealthy, but I could hear other girls' voices, shrill with excitement, so I assumed the theft had been accomplished.

The shower in the next room went off. The curtain was flung back on its rod. Then: silence. I could imagine Danya, Melanie, Zoe, and Eve standing outside the door, listening for sounds of distress, waiting to erupt into laughter. Sebastian had called Eve to tell her what was going on so she wouldn't worry, but I was still skeptical about her role in the whole enterprise.

Then came another knock on the wall. I opened the bathroom door and walked out of the office. Sure enough, the quartet was waiting, along with a locker room full of other girls. The hall door had been propped open, and several dozen guys hung in the doorway, George Garrison and Ben London among them, pushing to see over each other's shoulders. Everybody likes a good show. So we gave them one.

"Hey," I said. "What's everybody doing here?"

Danya gasped. "How . . . ?"

"I think they came to see me," Ms. Unger said as she lurched out of the shower room in three-inch pink heels, Danya's short, tight black dress stretched to the ripping point over her hips. She walked out into the locker room so the boys in the doorway could get a good look too. "Thank you, Danya, for lending me such nice clothes. I'm afraid I may have gotten the shoes a little wet though. And this side seam is beginning to open up just a bit."

For a moment no one said a word; then the boys began to hoot with laughter. The girls joined in too, and they weren't laughing at Ms. Unger. The joke was definitely on Danya.

Who was furious. She turned immediately on Eve. "You did this, didn't you? You little traitor! I knew I couldn't trust you!"

Eve opened her mouth, but no words came out.

"Hold on there, cowboy," Ms. Unger said, taking Danya by the arm. "I think you and I need to take that trip to the principal's office I was talking about. Grady, you'd better come too. The rest of you, go to your next class. The fun's over."

Danya gave Eve a parting look that would turn most mortals to stone, but Eve was looking at me, her woebegone expression begging forgiveness.

I followed Ms. Unger, who was now barefoot, holding the wrecked shoes in one hand and Danya's elbow in the other, as we padded down the hall to Dr. No Way's office. The kids we passed, late to class or clutching a pass of some kind, stared at Ms. Unger's bizarre outfit, then at her two unlikely companions. I wondered how long it would take before the entire school heard what had happened.

Ms. Unger swept right by the secretary and straight into the principal's office. I think he was playing solitaire on his computer, but he turned it off before I could be sure. He made us all sit down while Ms. Unger gave him the short version of what had just occurred and Danya interrupted with stupid excuses about how it was all just a joke and we were taking it way too seriously. I could see that No Way wanted to believe Danya—that would be the easiest solution. But Ms. Unger wasn't backing down.

"This was obviously an attempt to humiliate Grady. There were students jammed in the doorway waiting to see him emerge in a dress."

No Way turned his attention to me. "I was afraid something like this would happen if you perservered with this idea, Angela. I warned you."

"Dr. Ridgeway!" Ms. Unger stamped her bare foot. "I hope you aren't blaming Grady for this! He's not the one making trouble—he's just living his life as best he can. If you don't understand the problem here, I'll talk to someone who does. Like the superintendent. Or maybe the newspapers would be interested in this kind of discriminatory incident. Or even the ACLU! This is certainly a civil-liberties issue."

Ridgeway's complexion turned chalky, and his fingers bounced nervously on his desk. If I'd known Ms. Unger was going to turn out to be a saint, I would have made sure to get every speck of dog crap out of the crevices of her sneakers.

"Oh now, calm down, Ms. Unger," he said, his voice shaky. "Of course I see the gravity of the situation. It's just that . . . well, children can't be expected to understand these things. I mentioned to Angela—um, Grady—that she, or he, might do better to wait until he was older to address these issues. A child like Danya—"

"I'm not a child!" Danya said. "And anyway, my mother says it's creepy too. You don't just decide to change your sex!"

"Gender," I corrected her. She glared.

"It's the job of schools to educate children, is it not?" Ms. Unger said. "I think Danya—and maybe her mother, too—could use some educating."

Danya sat up very straight in her chair. "How dare you say anything about my mother! She's the vice president of a company! You're a gym teacher!"

Ms. Unger looked like she wanted to dropkick Danya the length of a football field, but No Way motioned with his hands for us to settle down. "I do agree with Ms. Unger that some punishment is in order here." He cleared his throat. "How about this? Danya, you'll have detention after school for the rest of this week."

Danya grumbled.

"Three days' suspension," Ms. Unger said calmly. "And it goes on her permanent record."

"It's not up to you!" Danya said, making an ugly face at her.

"Three days' suspension or I go to the newspapers," Ms. Unger said. "The rest of the students need to understand the importance of this."

No Way fidgeted. "Well, I don't know, Ms. Unger, that seems a bit harsh, don't you think?"

Ms. Unger stood patiently waiting.

"Fine," he said, sighing deeply. "Three days' suspension, beginning now. I'll call your mother."

Danya jumped up. "What? No! You can't call my mother!"

"Well, your father then."

"You can't call him, either!" And then, something I never thought I'd witness: Tears slid down Danya's cheeks. "You can't suspend me! You don't understand—my parents think I'm—I *can't* be suspended."

"Well, you are, cowboy," Ms. Unger said. "Get used to it."

No Way turned to Ms. Unger. "You and . . . *Grady* may leave now. And I would appreciate it if you'd put some shoes on, Ms. Unger. It sets a bad example for the students to see you dressed like that."

Ms. Unger swung the pink shoes up and plopped them down on No Way's desk. "Right. I'd hate to corrupt any of these fine minds. Danya, you can pick up your lovely dress in my office when you return on Friday. I'll be looking forward to having a little chat with you!"

For the first time I could remember, the smug, satisfied look that normally coated Danya Seifert's features was gone. She slumped back down in her chair, her complexion gray, looking like any other scared kid whose parents were about to be told the bad news.

I didn't know what to say to Ms. Unger as I followed her back down the hall. *You're my hero* seemed a little too gushy, even if it was true. I picked up my book bag in her office and made an attempt.

"Thank you for doing this, Ms. Unger. I don't know what I would have done . . ."

She shook her head. "No big deal, Grady. Thing is, you're going to need more support than just mine. How are your parents doing with it?"

"Okay. I mean, they had a hard time at first, but they're getting better about it. And I have friends here at school, too." *Well, one anyway.*

"That's great." She opened her desk drawer, took out a piece of paper with an address on it, and handed it to me. "I've been doing a little research for you. There's a GLBT group for teenagers that meets in Barrington a few times a month. That was the closest group I could locate—you might want to visit it sometime."

"Thanks. I might." I put the paper into a side pocket of my bag. "I'm actually not doing too badly, you know. I mean, most people don't hate me the way Danya does . . ."

"That girl hates herself. People that mean are uncomfortable in their own skins. Which doesn't excuse her behavior in the least."

"Yeah."

"You need a pass for your next class?"

"No, I've got lunch."

"Okay. Be careful, Grady."

"You mean because kids will tease me about this?"

"I mean because Danya will want revenge."

Chapter Sixteen

Sebastian and I had planned to walk to his house after school. We knew it would be a weird day, and we figured we'd kick back with a movie and some pizza. He'd gotten *Ghost World*, *Living in Oblivion*, and a French movie called *Ma Vie en Rose* for me to choose from. He'd seen them all already and obviously liked the idea that he was educating me. The French movie ("My Life in Pink") was about a little boy who liked to dress in girls' clothes. I wanted to see that sometime, but after a day like the one I'd just had, a dark comedy with Steve Buscemi seemed more appealing.

As we walked out the main entrance of the school, I saw Kita standing alone at the bottom of the stairs. Sebastian saw her too, and the possibility of sneaking by her without a word was lost. Not that I didn't want to speak to Kita—of course I did—but just seeing the back of her head from ten yards away made my stomach knot up like a bag of pretzels. Hadn't I had enough stress for one day?

"Hey, Kita!" Sebastian called out as we came down the stairs.

She swung around, her hair flying out like a dancer's dark skirt. "Hi, Sebastian," she said. "I was waiting to talk to you two—well, mostly to Grady. I heard about what happened today."

"Yeah," I said. "I guess everybody's heard by now."

Kita narrowed her eyes and made a fist. "Those stupid girls," she said. And then, as if she'd summoned them, two skinny girls in jeans that barely hung on their hip bones ran over to me.

"Excuse me," the braver of the two said. "Could I ask you a few questions for the school newspaper?"

I hesitated and Kita jumped in. "What kind of questions?"

"Um, well, like . . . are you planning to have a sex-change operation?" She stared at my crotch while the other girl made nervous noises in her throat.

"Well, I don't know," I answered honestly. "I've thought about it, but it's a big step. Maybe when I'm older—"

"Wait a minute—why is the school newspaper asking people such personal questions?" Kita wanted to know. "This isn't school news."

But my interrogator ignored her. "Well then, we were wondering, um, you know . . . I mean, we don't really get it. You know, how you *do* it. A boy who's not really a . . . you know, boy."

Kita and Sebastian and I stared at one another a few seconds, trying to make sense of the question. She wasn't really asking me *that*, was she?

"What is it you need to 'get'?" Kita asked them, her voice thick with disgust. "Are you really asking Grady how he has sex? I bet you aren't even *on* the school paper, are you? You're just a couple of nosy brats!"

The girls stared at her as she exploded. "Has anybody ever asked *you* that kind of question? Do you prefer big biceps or big dicks? Come on, girls! Don't you want to tell me all about your personal sexual choices?"

I think the brave girl swallowed her gum. "Jeez," she said. "Chill."

I stepped in front of Kita, partly to fight my own battle and partly so she wouldn't break the little people in half.

"Nobody ever knows what goes on between two people when they're alone, do they? All you know is what they tell you—and most people don't tell. What I am is a person who's capable of loving other people. That's all that matters."

Both girls turned around and stumbled off, looking embarrassed.

Kita grabbed my hand and squeezed it. "Grady, that was great," she said. "You told them, those creeps. What's wrong with people like that?"

I took a deep breath and shrugged. "They don't like me, I guess."

"They don't have to like you," she said loudly. "They just have to mind their own business!" Between the two of us we'd attracted a lot of attention. Kita noticed me looking around uncomfortably.

"Listen, I have my mother's car today. Let's get out of here—go get coffee or something. I want to talk to you. Oh, and you too, Sebastian. You should come too."

But Sebastian already had his escape plan in place. "Oh, I'd like to, but I promised my mother I'd go to the library and pick up this book right after school. They're holding it for her and she's really anxious to get it. You guys go get coffee. You can come over to my place afterward, Grady." He took off after the bogus book before we could protest.

A lot of kids saw me getting into Kita's car, and

I wondered what they were thinking. Kita was the definition of cool at Buxton Central High School. Not the kind of cool that cares about being cool, but *real* cool. Being seen with the local oddball might damage the reputations of certain pseudo-cool kids, but because Kita couldn't care less what people thought, it probably just enhanced her standing. What it might have done for me, I had no idea.

We didn't say much in the car—Kita drove carefully, and I wrote a little scene in my head.

GUM GIRL: So, like, how do trans . . . whatever-you-ares . . . have sex? I mean, 'cause you're so abnormal and all.

ME: Well, sex for us abnormals is very strange, as I'm sure you can imagine.

GUM GIRL: Ooh, yes, I'm imagining it!

ME: First of all, we have to be in the same room with the person we're having sex with.

GUM GIRL: [writing it down] Right. In the same room . . .

ME: And it really helps if we like each other a lot.

GUM GIRL: [still writing] Like . . . each . . . other . . .

ME: And then we touch each other's bodies in places where it feels good.

GUM GIRL: Feels . . . good . . . Hey, wait a minute.

This doesn't sound any different from regular sex!

ME: Really? I had no idea you normal folks did it that way too.

GUM GIRL: [suspiciously] Have you ever even had sex?

ME: Well, no, but I can imagine!

Kita parked in the lot behind Java King. As we walked in, the arm of her peacoat brushed against my down jacket. You would think with all those layers between us, I wouldn't even have noticed. You would be wrong. We ordered and took our drinks to a table in the back of the store.

Our butts had barely hit the chairs when Kita said, "That's what's wrong with guys like Ben and George, our big athletic *heroes*, dressing up like ugly girls and speaking in falsetto voices. It makes a joke out of something really serious."

"Gender dysphoria," I said, supplying the term they used on the online sites.

"Right. And that opens the door for the kind of cruelty Danya specializes in, or the insensitivity of those so-called newspaper reporters."

"I guess people feel threatened," I said. "So they make fun of the stuff they don't understand."

Kita shook her head. "How do you stand it,

Grady? How do you deal with people who are such idiots? Don't you get furious? Don't you just want to . . . to hurt them back?"

I thought about it. "People like those stupid newspaper girls are annoying, but it only really hurts me when somebody I care about does something crappy to me. I never liked Danya to begin with, so I can't get too worked up over her nastiness. But I've been really mad at Eve Patrick, because we were best friends practically our whole lives until she started hanging around with Danya. Now she acts like she hardly even knows me."

"That's terrible, Grady. I'd never speak to her again if I were you," Kita said.

"Well, but then she was the one who told me about Danya's plan today. She saved me from gross humiliation, so I guess I can't really hate her anymore."

Kita sighed and sipped her coffee. Her eyes were looking in my direction, but I was pretty sure she wasn't seeing me anymore. "It's always more complicated than you want it to be, isn't it? You want to be totally mad at somebody, but it's hard when you used to like them so much."

"Are we talking about Russ now?"

"No. Well, yes, I guess we are." She smacked

her cup down on the table. "He's so aggravating. One minute he's a sweet guy, all what-can-I-do-for-you-Kita, and the next minute he's completely selfish. He hurts my feelings and he doesn't even realize he did it. He's such a *guy*!"

"But girls can be hurtful too. Look at Eve. Look at Danya!"

"Yes, but girls *know* when they're being mean. Russell just walks all over me like it's his birthright. Like my plans or thoughts couldn't possibly be as important as his. Or like I'm his mother and he's getting away with something. It makes me crazy."

"I guess some guys do act that way. My little brother is kind of like that, but I don't think my dad is. Maybe they grow out of it."

As soon as I said that, I thought of my mother putting up with Dad's Christmas fuss all these years and him not really registering how much she hated it. As much as I adored my father, and even though he was usually nice about it, I had to admit that in our family he always got the last word. Was that sense of yourself as leader of the pack, as the one who was always right, programmed into men at the factory? And if so, did I have it? It didn't seem so. Maybe I'd have to rethink my placement on Sebastian's gender football field.

I pulled my mind back to Kita's troubles. "You know, Russ is basically a good guy. I think he does respect you, but maybe he doesn't know how to show it."

She snorted. "Well, it's too late now anyway—we broke up, remember?"

"You don't sound too happy with that decision though."

"I'll get used to it." She smiled. "You know, Grady, I think I could tell you spent most of your life as a girl even if I didn't already know it."

"You could?"

She nodded. "You pick up on things. You care about other people. You aren't just thinking about yourself all the time." She laughed. "Maybe if Russell had been a girl for a few years, we'd get along better."

I smiled, but not energetically. "Maybe. But there's got to be an easier way."

Her hand flew up to her mouth. "Oh, Grady, I didn't mean to make light of what you're going through. I'm so sorry. I would never want to hurt your feelings!" The hand that had recently covered her mouth reached up and ran along my cheekbone, sending out signals of delight throughout my body.

"I know," I said, but then I couldn't continue speaking because my brain short-circuited. Kita was staring soulfully into my eyes, caressing my face with the tips of her fingers. I couldn't help it; my eyes began to flicker down to the soft pink-brown of her lips, which seemed closer than they'd been just a second before.

"Grady, I really admire you," she said. "You're such a great person, and so, kind of, adorable." And then she kissed me. Kita Charles leaned across that little table and kissed me.

When she sat back again, smiling, I felt like I'd been smacked in the head with a fairy godmother's wand. Everything was different; everything was right; everything was perfect. I was, kind of, adorable.

I looked around the coffee shop to see if this miracle had been apparent to anybody else, but they were all reading newspapers and novels, sharing gossip and mainlining caffeine, completely unaware of the way in which one small event can change the whole world.

Afterward, Kita dropped me off at Sebastian's house. I arrived at the same moment as the pizza, but Sebastian was far more interested in me. He leaped around me like a puppy, begging for details.

"She kissed me" was all I said. What more was

there to say? Did she like me? Did she feel sorry for me? Did she regret it two seconds later? I had no idea.

Sebastian's mouth fell open. We ate pizza and decided to watch *Ma Vie en Rose* after all.

Chapter Seventeen

Ms. Unger was right about Danya wanting revenge, but, as it turned out, it wasn't revenge on me. I didn't hear about it from Eve herself; Wednesday night she called Sebastian and he called me.

Before launching into the story, he asked me what he'd been asking me constantly for two days. "Have you heard from Kita? Did you see her at school? Did she call you?"

"No, no, and no. It was just a spontaneous thing," I told him. "It didn't mean anything." But in my heart I hoped that wasn't true—I hoped the meaning of it would soon become obvious. If Kita's feelings for me were one quarter of what mine were for her, I would die happy. But I couldn't admit it, not yet.

I changed the subject. "So what's the story with Eve? Is she freaking out that Danya's mad at her?"

"Mad doesn't begin to describe it, Grady.

Apparently Danya and her minions are spreading the word that Eve is a lesbian and that you and she were girlfriends before she came to Buxton High. Eve is very upset."

I didn't want to hear it. "Why? What's the big deal? Being a lesbian is practically normal compared to me, right?"

"Come on, Grady. You can understand this. Eve is shy, and she's hardly made any friends at the high school except Danya's awful group of ninnies, who she hooked up with before she knew better. She's not a lesbian, and she doesn't want kids to think she is. You should get that—you want people to know who *you* really are."

I grumbled. "She had one friend when she got to the high school. She preferred to look for new ones."

"Grady, Eve feels really bad about all of that. You know she does. She never wanted to stop being your friend, but she was scared. She didn't mean to hurt you."

"Yeah, that whole thing backfired, didn't it? Anyway, how do you know so much about Eve's feelings?"

"I just talked to her for forty-five minutes. Look, she took a big chance telling you about Danya's trick. She must have known Danya would figure out who told you about it. Don't you think we owe her something in return?"

"'We'? *We* owe her?"

"Well, technically you do, but I'm willing to jump in too."

I sighed. "What am I supposed to do? Wear a sign around my neck that says, 'Eve is not a lesbian'? Go on the cable channel and declare, 'I did not have sex with that woman'?"

"That would be amusing," he said. "But, no. The first thing you could do is to be nicer to your old friend. She really needs you now."

I grunted. "Where was she when I needed her?"

Sebastian didn't answer for a minute, then he said. "She's been there, quietly. Some people are stronger than others, Grady. Be glad you're one of the strong ones."

That Sebastian. I never knew what he was going to say next. Was I a strong person? Stronger than Eve—*that* I could see. Eve had always been the kind of person who preferred to follow carefully in someone else's footprints. Mine, until her unfortunate alliance with Danya Siefert. But if "strong" meant stable, steady, determined—did those adjectives define me? Not every day they didn't, but sometimes, and more often as the days passed.

"I have to go," Sebastian said, interrupting my reverie. "You *are* going to have my paper proofread by tomorrow, aren't you? I need to fix any problems you find and get it turned in by Thursday."

"Yeah, I was just about to start it when you called," I lied.

"Good. Don't forget to bring it to school tomorrow."

"I won't," I promised.

After we hung up, I retrieved the stoplight-parrotfish paper from my book bag. It was a ridiculous notion: me, proofreading a paper for Sebastian, the A-plus English student who read Shakespeare for fun. I knew it was just a ruse to get me to read the paper, of which he was very proud.

"The Fascinating World of the Stoplight Parrotfish" was twenty-six pages long with an additional four pages of footnotes and a two-page bibliography. I suspected Sebastian would say he enjoyed doing the work.

> Stoplight parrotfish are commonly found among the coral reefs in the tropical waters of the Florida Keys, the Bahamas, the Gulf of Mexico, and the Caribbean Sea.

More about their size, life span, etc., etc.

> Parrotfish exhibit three adaptations that set them apart from other fish. First, they have a set of teeth in the back of their throats called pharyngeal teeth, which they use to grind up coral and extract from it the algae known as zooxanthellae, a necessary nutrient for the fish.

Information about the excretion of the ground-up coral, which eventually becomes beautiful white Caribbean beaches. More than I wanted to know about where sand comes from.

> A second unusual characteristic of this fish is that it secretes and surrounds itself with a mucus cocoon at night to protect itself from predators.

And what that smells and tastes like. Scientists are a hardy breed.

> But the third parrotfish adaptation is perhaps the most fascinating. Depending on fluctuations in population density, these fish may change their gender from female to male.

Okay, this is the part for me. I'm liking it that the young female is an undistinguished gray with a red belly, but it turns a beautiful green with a golden-yellow stripe down its face when it becomes male.

> Nature creates many variations, and gender ambiguity is not unusual. It is normally a device to allow reproduction to succeed. Particularly among fish, gender can be quite flexible. In fact, reef fish that do not change gender are in the minority.

Okay, that is pretty cool. If only I were a better swimmer.

> Gender shifting occurs only when it's necessary for survival.

Now, *that* I can relate to. It's necessary that I no longer live as a female. Necessary for my mental survival, if not actually all that great for my day-to-day physical life.

The paper goes on to tell about the advantages of being able to switch genders. As Sebastian told me earlier, the females who change to males are called supermales and are dominant over the regular old *born* males. Which is a fantasy I haven't even bothered to imagine. It does, however, seem that the only purpose for the gender changing is to ensure rapid reproduction, thereby allowing the species a better chance of survival. So what's my excuse? Having babies has nothing to do with my reasons for wanting to live as a male. In fact, it may—probably will—hinder my chances of ever reproducing. Sebastian meant well, but alas, I am just not a fish.

Still, I read on to the end, finding and marking one missing comma and one instance of "the" mistyped as "tha," both mistakes I'm sure Sebastian made purposely so I'd feel useful.

And then, the last page:

> Matthew Grober of Georgia State University has measured the number of cells producing isotocin (a hormone involved in reproduction) in female fish that change gender.

Blah, blah, blah. Then:

> "The part of the brain that controls sexuality is the same in all animals, including fish and humans," said Grober. "And animals that change sex in a matter of days, like the bluebanded goby, are ideal systems to understand what drives maleness and femaleness across species."

And finally, Sebastian's summation:

> Perhaps the study of the stoplight parrotfish and other gender-switching reef fish will eventually shed light on the mysteries of human gender, enabling us to understand what makes a person—both in body and in mind—male or female, or even a little bit of each.

I was momentarily stunned. There were people actually studying these things—what makes somebody male or female. *Oh, Mr. Grober,* I thought, *please keep doing that research! Because if you understand these things, maybe I will too, and maybe my parents will, and eventually so will everybody else. And if you can't do it, Mr. Grober, how about turning it over to Sebastian Shipley? He's one smart kid.*

SEBASTIAN: [into a microphone] Now that I've conquered the problem of speaking to fish, I will attempt to translate for you the words of my devoted helper, a stoplight parrotfish I call Malachite due to his astounding coloration. In fact, the color might more accurately be called aquamarine or even turquoise, but I chose the name for its classical quality. Greetings, Malachite!

MALACHITE: Up yours, Shipley. My name is Frank and you know it.

SEBASTIAN: Malachite sends his greetings to us all. Now, would you tell the audience, please, Malachite, what it felt like to change your gender from that of female to that of supermale.

MALACHITE: Felt like a million bucks, lemme tell you. At last I could stop being barefinned and pregnant all the time. I put on those super-tights and I was the alpha dogfish! These days I leave the toilet seat up and everything!

SEBASTIAN: [hesitates a moment] Ah . . . Malachite says the transition was miraculous. He feels that becoming a male fulfills his biological imperative.

MALACHITE: I said that?

SEBASTIAN: Can you tell us, is there anything you miss about being a female?

MALACHITE: Oh, sure, let's see. I miss sitting around in the algae all day long with a bunch of fishlets hanging on my scales yelling, "Mommy, I don't want to sleep in my mucus sack tonight!" Or, "Do I have to eat zooxanthellae for dinner again?" Oh, yeah, it's a ball being female.

SEBASTIAN: Malachite says, no, being male is just fine with him.

MALACHITE: You can say that again, cowboy!

"Hello?" From the thickness of her voice, I presumed Eve had already been crying. It could be a soggy conversation.

"It's me," I said, as I had so often during the past twelve years.

She sniffed. "Oh! It's you! I guess Sebastian told you to call me."

"He didn't *tell* me to. He mentioned that you were upset, that Danya's been spreading stories about the two of us. What a surprise."

She let out a deep breath. "Why did I ever start hanging around with her? She's horrible. I know, you told me, but Angie . . ." She stopped and grunted. "Grady, Grady, Grady. It's not that I don't want to use your new name—it's just that you've been Angie since we were little kids. It's hard to think of you as somebody else. It's confusing. What if I suddenly became Beverly or something? Could you stop calling me Eve overnight?"

"Beverly? That would be hard, I admit."

"Anyway, I'm sorry about the way I've been acting. I felt terrible about it—really, I felt sick—but once I started hanging around with Danya and her friends, it was like I was stuck or something. If I didn't do everything she wanted me to, she turned on me. I didn't know how to get out of it, and I was scared of her. God, I'm so tired of being a big chicken all the time. I wish I could be more like you."

"Hey, you told me about Danya's trick. That wasn't something a big chicken would do."

"Are you kidding? I was terrified!"

"But you told me anyway, and now you're paying for it. And I . . . I just wanted to say thank you."

It occurred to me that for the past month or more I'd been waiting for Eve to understand what was going on with me, and to forgive me for it. But now that seemed backward. Maybe it was my job to understand what was going on with her, and to forgive her for that.

After a long silence Eve said, "So, are you not so mad at me anymore?"

I laughed. "Yes, I'm not so mad at you anymore."

"Thank God! I missed you so much . . . Grady!"

"I missed you too," I admitted.

"At least one good thing came out of all this," Eve said. "At least we got to know Sebastian Shipley."

"We" did?

"He is such a great guy, don't you think?" Eve continued. "I mean, I know he probably just asked me because of those silly rumors Danya started, but still, it made me so happy, I started to cry!"

I was a few steps behind her. "What are you talking about? What did Sebastian ask you?"

She giggled rather uncontrollably. "Didn't he tell you? He asked me to the Winter Carnival dance!"

Chapter Eighteen

When I came downstairs Thursday morning, Mom was sitting at the kitchen table, her hair unbrushed, her chin cupped in both hands. She was wearing her ratty old bathrobe that had lost its belt before Charlie was born.

"Mom's sick," Charlie announced as he refilled his bowl with red and green cereal. "I'm going to Dan's house. It's our last day of school until January second!"

"You're sick?" I asked.

She nodded. "Can't drive. You can have the car. Take your sister."

"Is it the flu?"

"I guess. I'm going back to bed." She scooted her chair away from the table and pushed herself carefully to her feet.

"Should I make you some tea?"

She motioned no. "Can't eat." Then, as she shuffled to the stairs, she suddenly remembered something. "Oh, damn! I didn't take in any clothes for you for Saturday night. Or let anything out for Charlie either. I was going to sew today, but now I don't have the strength."

"Don't worry about it," I assured her. "It won't matter."

She leaned against the wall. "Your dad will be upset. You know he likes his pageant to be perfect."

"Oh, it'll be perfect," I said, grinning. "Just wait."

"Just the *idea* of having to cook a turkey . . . ugh. I hope nobody else gets this, or we'll have to cancel the whole thing." She sounded vaguely hopeful as she trudged upstairs.

"Hey, if I'm not Tiny Tim this year, does that mean I don't get the candy?" Charlie asked, taking a brief pause from inhaling sugar.

"That's right. You have forfeited your right to the licorice and peppermints."

"So I'm just getting those stupid socks again?"

"What difference does it make? You still get your real presents the next day."

He frowned. "I know, but I like opening presents in the window and acting real happy about them. It's hard to be happy about *socks*!"

"Just pretend you open the box and a dog jumps out," I told him. "It's called Method acting."

*

Laura and I were almost late getting to school because she was talking to Jason on the phone.

"You'll see him in ten minutes!" I said. "If we actually leave the house now!"

She finally hung up and followed me out to the car. She didn't seem too upset about Mom's illness, or about my driving her to school in broad daylight either. In fact, now that Jason had invited her to the Winter Carnival dance, Laura didn't seem to be upset about anything.

"It's supposed to snow tomorrow," she said dreamily as we drove along.

"You don't like snow," I reminded her. "You don't like cold weather or winter or any month between October and March."

She laughed. "Oh, Grady, don't be silly. That was when I was a kid. Snow is . . . romantic."

Romantic? Laura obviously had visions of Jason Kramer picking her up in his one-horse open sleigh, the mare prancing, the harness bells jingling, snowflakes catching daintily in her eyelashes. She'd blocked out the more likely scenario of having to wade through slush in her new suede shoes and then wait for the heater to kick in in Jason's father's car.

Still, I was glad to see that having a gender-switching sibling hadn't actually ruined my sister's life. She had friends, she had a boyfriend, she had her *Doctor Zhivago* dreams.

And she still had the ability to surprise me. "I am *so* glad Danya got suspended. You know, a lot of people really hate her," Laura said.

"You are? They do?"

"Of course I am. Grady, she tried to humiliate you in front of the whole school!" she said, as though I might be unaware of that fact. "Everybody thinks she's awful. She's so manipulative. We're all tired of her getting away with it."

We're all tired? Everybody thinks she's awful? Suddenly my sister, the freshman, was the mouthpiece for all of Buxton Central High School? "Eve isn't the first person she's told lies about, you know—she's hurt a lot of people. I mean, if it came down to choosing between you or Danya, most kids would much rather be your friend."

"Thanks," I said. "I guess I'll take that as a compliment."

"Really, Grady, most kids think it's pretty cool that you aren't afraid to be who you really are. I mean, they're a little confused about how it happened, but they think it's cool that you just put it right out there. 'I'm a boy now—deal with it!' This girl in my art class even told me she thinks you're cute."

I stared at my sister, whose body had obviously been taken over by a very sympathetic alien. She was smiling contentedly and staring out the car window at her own bright future. Never mind that two weeks ago she despised me, certain that my behavior would destroy her high-school experience—she was happy enough to claim me now. Did I have Jason Kramer to thank for this? Whatever. I decided to just shut up and appreciate it.

I didn't catch up to Sebastian until lunch, at which time I slid my tray onto the corner table and began a barrage of questions.

"You asked Eve to the dance? When did you decide to do that? You didn't even tell me!"

His smile was large and sappy. "I like her," he said.

"You *like* her? What does that mean?"

"Sorry, I thought you spoke English."

"Well, when did this—"

"Yesterday, after I talked to you. I suddenly thought, 'Why not? All she can say is no—that won't kill me.' And I figured she might want to show up with a guy to erase the label Danya was pinning on her. And I guess she did."

I glowered. "That's not why she's going with you."

"Why do you say that? Have you talked to her?"

I nodded. "Last night. She was very happy you asked her. She thinks you're a 'great guy.'"

"She does? Wow." He stared off into the distance.

I leaned over and drummed a finger against his temple. "Maybe you've forgotten—we have to *film* the dance. How can you have a date?" I wasn't sure why I was acting so crabby about this, but Sebastian's sudden interest in Eve had caught me off balance.

He waved away my objections. "Once we get the cameras set up, we don't have to man them every minute. There'll be three of us, you know, and you and Russ don't have dates. Do you?"

"You know I don't. And Kita says she's going alone, so I don't think Russ does either."

"So, no problem. You guys can watch the cameras while I dance with Eve."

Yeah, no problem, except for the forlorn feeling of abandonment I was trying to fight off. I'd just gotten my oldest friend back, and now she was hooking up with my best *new* friend. I couldn't help wondering where that left me.

Suddenly Sebastian slapped my arm, hard. "There she is," he said, then stood and waved to

Eve. She'd been standing in the middle of the cafeteria, holding a tray and looking lost. She couldn't sit with Zoe and Melanie anymore: Even though Danya was suspended, they wouldn't dare allow her at their table. And kids were staring at her, watching what she'd do next, a situation I was sure was among her worst nightmares.

Sebastian to the rescue. "Eve!" he called out, not worried in the slightest about who might stare at him.

Relief flooded her face when she saw who was calling her. She zipped over and slid into the empty chair Sebastian brought over to our tiny table.

"Thanks," she said, her back to the rest of the room. "God, this is awful. Is everybody still looking at me?"

"No," Sebastian lied.

"Kind of," I said. "Try to ignore them. In a few days they'll forget all about it. Look, they hardly even stare at *me* anymore."

I'd meant that as a gentle joke, but Eve started to tear up—she was on the verge anyway. "Grady, I feel so terrible about what I did to you. You're probably thinking that I deserve this. I do deserve it."

Sebastian looked frightened by her sudden dampness, but I was used to it. "Hey, look at me,

Eve. *Do not cry.* That will just give the idiots more to gossip about."

She nodded and took a deep breath, trying to get herself under control.

"I'm not mad at you anymore," I said. "And I don't think anybody deserves the crap that Danya dishes out. We're both going to stand up to her and show her that she doesn't have the power to hurt us. Right?"

"Right." She sniffled a little and sighed. "What would I do without you, Grady? You're the best."

Sebastian's tentative smile was hardening into shoe leather. I could tell he was feeling as left out as I had been a few minutes before. "Yes," he said, "Grady is definitely the best."

"You both are," Eve insisted. "You're the two best guys in this school!"

Guys. I think Eve was surprised at the ease with which she'd said it too, but I was completely overwhelmed.

This time Sebastian was the one to lean across the table. "Grady!" he said. "*Do not cry!*"

Chapter Nineteen

Friday was one of those days when the teachers pretty much give up trying to teach anything and just show movies and pass out cookies. It was the last day before winter vacation week and the day of the Winter Carnival dance; the last thing anybody wanted to think about was *Jane Eyre* or trigonometry. You could be sure that six or seven girls would have to leave school early for "a dentist appointment," which everyone knew was code for "the hair salon."

I can't say I was really feeling the excitement of these upcoming events. Yeah, I'd be going to the dance, but only to shoot video and watch my two best friends become a couple. Of course, Kita would be there too, but I didn't want to get my hopes up about what that might mean—it wasn't too likely she was going to smooch with me in front of the entire school. And the night after that

I could look forward to destroying one of my father's grand passions in life. Ho, ho, ho. Merry Christmas.

Russ Gallo wasn't in a celebratory mood either. In TV Production he stood behind me making little grunting noises while I edited the footage from the chorus recital. I was more than a little nervous, wondering if anyone had told him about me getting into the car with Kita earlier in the week. Or . . . anything else.

"Man, I just don't get it," he said finally. "I went to the damn concert! I sat through the whole thing, and I hate that kind of singing. All those sopranos warbling around trying to find the right note. And then she doesn't even appreciate it! What does she expect of me?"

Was I supposed to answer that? "You mean Kita?" I said. *Duh.*

"Yeah, Kita! I was there—you saw me!"

I nodded. "But you didn't exactly enthuse over the performance, Russ. I mean, singing must be pretty important to her."

He shrugged. "I guess so. But does that mean I have to love it? I showed up—there were several other things I would rather have done that night."

"Well, showing up is sort of the minimal

requirement. Did you tell her you'd rather be doing something else?"

He sighed. "Maybe. I don't know. She's always saying I don't understand her, that I don't try hard enough. I *do* try, but I still don't understand her. I don't understand *girls*."

"I heard you broke up." I was trying hard to say nothing while still saying something. I'd already given up trying to edit the video.

"Did she tell you that? I don't want to break up with her—she's just being crazy again."

I cleared my throat and dared to look at Russ. "So, you still . . . like her?"

He ran his fingers through his hair as if he were plowing a field. "Man, I love her. She's beautiful and smart and just . . . awesome. But she drives me insane!"

That I could understand. "Yeah, Kita is pretty amazing."

Russ pulled up a chair. "Look, you've gotten to know her pretty well recently. And I know she likes you. So, I was just wondering . . . has she said anything about me? I mean, what am I supposed to do to get her back? I really miss her, Grady! What do you think I should do?"

For God's sake, Russ wanted advice from me on getting back together with the girl I was in love with! How did this happen? Was there a spot right in the middle of Sebastian's football field for *non*-sexuals? The gender-free? People who everybody felt comfortable telling their sad stories to, who could fill in for either a male or a female, whatever the situation demanded? People you wouldn't mind if your girlfriend kissed?

Still, the more I imagined that field, the more I knew I did belong there, right on the fifty-yard line, far from Scarlett and Beyoncé, far from Bruce. And maybe that was a good thing. Even if capital-M Man and capital-W Woman weren't goals I was likely to reach—were those the only acceptable goals? I was a boy who had once been a girl. I was some of each. Which was beginning to feel okay.

"I know," Russ whined. "I sound like a fool. But I don't want to lose her, Grady. I really don't." His miserable, sad eyes appealed to me.

So, I told him. "Kita thinks you don't really value her or her opinions. She thinks you're selfish. And you treat her as if she weren't as important as you."

"What? She's totally important to me!" His eyes were round as he took in what I was saying. "She thinks I'm selfish? She told you that?"

I nodded. "She thinks it's a male chauvinist thing. You know, testosterone poisoning."

"Wow." Russ leaned way back in his chair the way guys with long legs always do, without fear of falling over backward. "That's weird, because I don't feel that way at all. I mean, I don't even know how men are supposed to act. I'm just winging it. And sometimes I think I'm not fooling anybody anyway—they all know what a big sissy wimp I really am."

I was still trying to process Russ Gallo thinking he was a big sissy wimp, when he suddenly righted his chair, looking chagrined. "I'm sorry, Grady. I shouldn't be complaining to you about all this. I know you have your own stuff going on. It's just that you're an easy person to talk to."

"That's okay," I said, and it really was. "If anybody knows how hard it is to figure out how to be a man, it's me."

He nodded. "I guess that's true. Anyway, I'd never tell all that stuff to any of my *guy* friends. Even if they felt that way, I doubt they'd admit it. Guys don't."

"Sometimes I think—" I began, then hesitated. Could I really say this to a teenage male?

"What?" Russ wanted to know.

What the hell. "Sometimes I wish we didn't have to be one thing or the other. You know, male or female. I wish there wasn't that big division between the two. Does that make any sense?"

I could tell he wasn't sure what I meant, so I continued. "If we could each just be wherever we were on the football field—"

"What football field?" Now he was really lost.

Too much to explain. I tried again. "For example, you say you're afraid people will think you're a sissy wimp if they catch you not acting all masculine or something. But why are those the only two possibilities? Why do you have to be either macho or a sissy? Those are stereotypes anyway. Why can't you just be whoever you are?"

Russ was mulling it over. "Huh. I never thought about it like that. That's kind of true. You know, I think I'm going to apologize to Kita tonight at the dance. I hate for her to think I'm just some macho jerk."

I got up from the editing chair. "Good luck with Kita tonight." I sounded so sincere, I felt like smacking myself. No matter how much I liked Russ, his good luck was my misfortune. I left him there, thinking it all over, as I wandered off into midfield.

It was already snowing as I maneuvered our Toyota toward home, slipping around a bit on the crappy tires. At least the snow covering those old teddy bears on the lawn made them seem a little cleaner, although I imagined in the long run the dampness would only enhance their odor.

Our mailbox was so crammed with stuff, the door on it was hanging open. There, amidst the twenty-odd Christmas cards, the circulars from Wal-Mart, and the catalogs from Pottery Barn, was a package for me. My undershirt binder! I could hardly wait to get out of my terrible tight bandage and try it on. Thank God, I'd be able to breathe again without rib damage.

"Finally!" Laura said as I came through the door with the mail pile. She had baby Michael on her shoulder and was jiggling him wildly as he cried. "Where have you been?"

"I told you, I had to load up the camera equipment from the studio. Did you get a ride with Mira? How come Michael's here?"

"Because Aunt Gail is here, obviously. She's going to do my hair for tonight, but she's also taking care of Mom, who's been upstairs puking all day."

"Gee, thanks for the visual," I said.

"I can't wait to get out of this disease-infested hovel!" She handed Michael to me as though his damp diaper and wet cheeks were signs of leprosy.

"Could you be a little more dramatic? Where

are the clean diapers?" I could see the baby was beginning to melt down.

Laura pointed to a corner of the kitchen where Aunt Gail had deposited enough infant paraphernalia to open a day-care center. "There. I'm going upstairs to take a *long* shower so I don't smell like vomit and baby pee when Jason shows up!"

By the time I found the diapers, the baby wipes, and a clean towel to lay Michael on, Aunt Gail was coming downstairs. Her tread on the stairs was slow, and I imagined she was tired.

"Sweetheart!" she said when she saw me. "You don't have to do that! I'll change him."

"That's okay," I said. "I don't mind. I hear you've been having quite a day with Mom already. How is she?"

"Asleep, finally. The worst is over, but she'll feel like hell for a day or two. This flu is a bad one. Thank God Michael already had it so I don't have to worry about him. I hope the rest of us don't get it. Keep washing your hands."

I had to smile. Our whole family were inveterate hand washers because of Aunt Gail's constant stories of contagion.

Michael stopped bawling the minute the wet diaper was off. He stared up at me as I wiped him off and slipped the clean pad under him. I couldn't help but notice his little penis, which at this point in his life was of no more interest to him than a hand or an ear. I hoped that by the time he did understand what it meant, he'd be happy with the equipment he'd gotten at birth, or—less likely—that the world would have changed so dramatically that it wouldn't matter all that much.

Aunt Gail made us both cups of tea, and we sat at the kitchen table. Michael nursed greedily for five minutes and then conked out. Gail couldn't seem to wrench her eyes away from him, as though she still, after a month, couldn't believe that he was really hers.

She noticed me staring at her and said, "I know it seems crazy, this mother-child love thing. I never got it either when your mom tried to tell me. Thank God I finally took her advice and just jumped into it."

"*Her* advice?"

"Sure. She did all the research for me on sperm banks and everything. She just couldn't abide the idea that I'd go through life without having a child. She always told me how life-changing it was for her to have children and how much she adored you guys, even if you did drive her nuts sometimes." She looked back down at

Michael. "You know how I hate to admit it, but this time my sister was right."

I sipped my tea. "Do you think Mom still feels that way? That having kids is so great?"

"Why wouldn't she?"

"I mean, do you think I've . . . disappointed her?"

I figured Aunt Gail would just say, "Of course not!" because she felt like she had to, and I guess maybe that was why I asked her the question. I was in the mood for some unconditional love. But she didn't. I could tell she was really thinking about her answer.

"Grady," she said finally, "if your mother found out you were taking drugs, she would be disappointed. If you were flunking out of school, she'd be disappointed. But, all you're doing is figuring out who you are. I'll admit, changing gender is not something most teenagers go through, and your mom is confused by it, maybe even shocked, but not disappointed. Just last week she said to me, 'I don't know where Grady gets the courage.' She's proud of you, honey. She really is."

Fortunately, Charlie came banging through the door then, so I could slip a finger up unobtrusively and wipe away a stray tear.

"That Daniel can be so dumb!" he said, throwing his coat on the floor. "He wants us to do math problems, even though we're on vacation! He *likes* arithmetic!"

"Pick up your coat," I told him.

Aunt Gail put a finger to her lips. "Keep it down a little, Charlie. Your mom is sleeping." Of course, Michael was sleeping too, and I knew Gail was enjoying the peacefulness.

Charlie whispered as loudly as possible, while flinging his coat onto a hook, "I wish I had a brother to play with. Or Michael was older. Or I could go to regular school and meet some normal kids. Daniel is weird."

It was true that Daniel and Charlie weren't a perfect match, but they usually got along well enough. I wondered if Charlie would be less of a couch potato if he went to public school and had more friends. It hadn't occurred to me before that my loud, lazy, sometimes obnoxious brother might actually be lonely.

"Too bad Mom's so allergic to dogs," I said.

"Oh man, I want a dog *so much*," Charlie whined.

"You know, there are some dogs that are less likely to cause an allergic reaction," Aunt Gail said. "They don't shed like most dogs do."

"Probably those ugly little hairless ones," Charlie said, slumping into a chair, discouraged.

"I'm not sure. I've never looked into it." Gail stared back into her baby's face and in seconds forgot we were even there.

Chapter Twenty

Sebastian didn't have his driver's license yet, so I offered to chauffeur the three of us to the dance through the winter wonderland. I picked up Eve first, since she lived so close. She climbed in the front seat, smiled, and said, "Hi, Grady," but her voice was louder than normal, and I could tell she was really nervous. Which made me feel weird—and sad. Could things ever be the same between us after all that had happened?

We said nothing for about three minutes, and then Eve began to speak. "I'm sorry that—"

I waved my hand in her face. "Look, Eve, you can stop apologizing to me. I know you're sorry. It was a big mistake and you feel terrible about it. Let's just try to forget it, can we?"

Eve stared at me, then burst out laughing.

"What?"

"I was just going to say I was sorry you had to drive in this crummy weather."

"Oh." I felt kind of stupid, but also relieved. I laughed too. "So, you think maybe *I'm* the one who needs to forget about it?"

She shook her head. "I don't think either one of us will ever forget about it. But it's so good to be able to laugh with you, Grady. Do you think we can be friends again?"

All my anger and sadness gurgled right down the drain. "I hope so. I've really missed you!"

"Me too!" Eve was smiling so big, I was afraid she'd crack her cheekbones.

"So, what are you wearing?" I asked because I knew she'd appreciate telling me.

She opened her coat to show me. "That red velvet dress I got last Christmas, remember?"

"The one you begged your mother to buy you but then never wore? And she kept saying, 'I told you it was a waste of money'?"

"That's the one! I didn't have any place fancy enough to wear it. She got so mad, remember? She wanted me to wear it to church, just so I'd make use of it, but I knew I should save it for something special. And now it will always be the dress I wore to the Winter Carnival dance when I was a sophomore in high school."

Talking to Eve about our shared past, I felt like I was suddenly breathing deeply again. I hadn't lost my entire childhood—it was still alive, in my memory and in Eve's.

We were yakking away by the time we got to Sebastian's. When he got in the car, I didn't pull out right away, and Eve didn't move from the front seat. We just kept talking about Daniel and Charlie and how they didn't seem to be enjoying being homeschooled anymore now that the other three of us were in public school. How Charlie, especially, seemed to feel he was missing out on something. It was such a relief to be able to talk about stuff like that with Eve again.

Sebastian cleared his throat noisily. "Excuse me, Eve, would you mind sitting back here with me? I mean, since you're my date."

"Oh, sure!" She giggled, then got out of the front seat and into the back. So I drove and let the two of them talk and get better acquainted. It was more comfortable than I'd expected, being a third wheel. Still, a vehicle with four wheels was what you really wanted to drive. If Kita had been sitting up front next to me, the evening would have been complete.

Eve helped us carry in the camera equipment, though we both told her she didn't have to, dressed as she was. But it was clear even wet shoes couldn't ruin her mood: She had a date, and she had her best friend back. Even the idea that Danya might show up—which Sebastian mentioned cautiously—didn't throw her.

"I hope she does," Eve said. "I'll be happy to glare at her scornfully, the way she looks at everybody else."

Russ came in shortly after we did, looking slightly frazzled, but still very cool in a suit and tie. Sebastian was dressed up too. He even looked slightly taller, and I noticed he had on shoes with higher heels than his usual sneakers. Eve had worn fancy red and gold flats so she wouldn't be taller than Sebastian; the two of them looked pretty adorable together.

Choosing my outfit had not been simple. I don't own a suit, so that wasn't a possibility. I didn't have a date, so I could have gotten away with wearing the typical geek-who's-not-a-part-of-the-festivities costume of jeans and a T-shirt. And if I'd just intended to hide out behind the camera all night, I would have. But Kita would be there, and maybe we'd talk, and I didn't want to look like a bum. So I ended up wearing a dark-green dress shirt borrowed from Dad's closet—with, of course, the new, more comfortable binder underneath—and a pair of black cords. The shirtsleeves were long, but I usually rolled them up anyway. When

I dared to look in the mirror, the effect seemed pretty good, and I left the house feeling better in my clothes—and in my skin—than I had in ages.

By the time we got the third camera ready to go, the one aimed at the stage, the band had finished its sound check, and the first couples were arriving. Taping a dance is actually pretty boring. Three hours of people having fun. Or pretending to have fun, hoping they resemble Shakira or at least one of her backup dancers. Or sticking out their tongues at the camera. Or being photographed in front of a blue sheet hung with paper snowflakes. You could take some shots of the band, of course. But band videos were pretty stock footage too. And this band was not Green Day.

I positioned myself behind the camera nearest the entrance so I could watch the kids come in, from the freshmen pushing forward in eager clumps—mostly girls—giggly and excited, on up to the seniors, cool and coupled up, dressed in outfits that wouldn't look out of place at the Academy Awards. They stared at me, too, some of them, and then smiled or frowned or looked away. Which I figured is probably what they would have done anyway, even if I was still a girl.

FRESHMAN GIRL: Ooh, look, there's that girl, Angela.

SENIOR GIRL: You mean that boy, Grady.

FRESHMAN GIRL: Yeah, that's so weird. How did that happen?

SENIOR GIRL: [shrugs] He just changed. No biggie.

FRESHMAN GIRL: Oh, sure, no biggie. I know that.

SENIOR GIRL: When you're my age, nothing shocks you anymore.

FRESHMAN GIRL: Right. [pause] I like your dress.

SENIOR GIRL: So do I.

FRESHMAN GIRL: This is the first dance I've ever been to.

SENIOR GIRL: They're all alike.

FRESHMAN GIRL: What if nobody asks me to dance? I'll be so embarrassed.

SENIOR GIRL: That's quite likely to happen. Boys can't dance. Especially freshman boys.

FRESHMAN GIRL: Can I dance with my girlfriends?

SENIOR GIRL: Only if you dance in a big circle. Or if you're a lesbian.

FRESHMAN GIRL: Oh, I'm not a . . .

SENIOR GIRL: I don't really care, sweetheart. I really don't.

FRESHMAN GIRL: [suddenly lost in thought] At least I don't think I am . . . although now that you mention it . . .

SENIOR GIRL: [wandering off toward the ladies' bathroom] I need a cig. Ta, babes.

I was enjoying making up dialogue for the partygoers as I taped them entering the tinfoil-starred and plastic-snowy ballroom. I almost didn't recognize Laura in her floor-length black-and-white dress and carefully assembled hair. The exceptionally tall, skinny kid with her was obviously Mr. Popularity: The minute they walked into the room, other freshmen started to gather around them. I was glad for Laura. This was the kind of high-school experience she'd probably dreamed of. It might not last forever, but at least she'd have good memories of this night. I videotaped her smiling at Jason, laughing with friends. Someday she'd be happy I had.

And then, finally, *she* came in, hugging her coat tightly around her body. I didn't move a muscle, just stared at her until she felt it and turned to smile at me. She was with one of her girlfriends, but they went separate ways after they hung up their coats. Kita was wearing a short coral-colored dress that made her dark skin seem to glow. Just as I leaped to my feet, I saw Russ bearing down on her from across the room, his arms opening as he approached.

I wished I could hear what they were saying. Kita wasn't acting too happy to see him, but she wasn't ignoring him either. He was gesturing to the back hallway, and I knew he wanted to talk to her alone. Before going with him, she turned around and waved at me. Did that mean anything?

The crowd got bigger. With Russ gone, Sebastian and I moved from camera to camera, trying to get some decent shots of the dance floor before it got too mobbed. I spotted a gawky, curly-haired girl in a blue dress hopping up and down in a circle of other self-conscious girls, and I decided she had to be Wilma's niece Katy, so I took a nice long shot of the whole group. I owed Wilma that, at least.

After fifteen minutes or so, Russ returned with a grin on his face—which made my stomach lurch as if I were tumbling through white water on a small raft. I didn't have time to scout the room for Kita, because Sebastian and Eve wanted to dance, so he abandoned camera duty.

After forty-five minutes, the place was already starting to look pretty straggly. The dancers were as sweaty as track stars, and girls' hairdos were coming undone. Ties and shoes had been stripped off, and decorative streamers had been pulled down and wound around waists and necks.

Most of the tablecloths had red punch stains on them, and the floor crackled with crunched-up pretzels and chips. Same old, same old.

When Sebastian came back, he said, "Eve is talking to Zoe and Melissa. Can you believe it? They're mad at Danya too. Only they were too chicken to say anything until Eve took the first step and obviously lived to tell the story. Now they're acting like they weren't even involved with the whole scheme to humiliate you."

"Maybe they weren't. It's hard to tell with cowards."

Sebastian laughed. "Yeah, I guess. Did you see Danya come in?"

"No, is she here?"

He nodded. "Over by the food table."

I craned my neck to see her. "Is that her in the short black dress?" I asked.

"Yup."

"She looks . . . smaller or something," I said.

"I think that's because she's alone. Nobody's talking to her. Without a posse following her around, she doesn't seem so powerful."

"What do you mean, 'Nobody's talking to her'?"

He gave me a long look. "I mean, no one in

the room is speaking the English language or any other language in a conversational way with her. Got it?"

"Really?"

But then, as we watched from across the room, a girl approached Danya, put a hand on her arm, and began to speak.

"Is that Kita?" Sebastian asked.

"Oh my God."

We couldn't hear anything over the band noise, but it seemed like Kita was yelling at Danya. People nearby stopped dancing and turned around to see what was going on. After a few minutes, Danya pulled away and ran across the floor, retreating to the usual party sanctuary, the girls' bathroom.

"Wow, what do you think happened there?" Sebastian said.

"I don't know. Can I go talk to her? Russ is here—the two of you can handle the cameras, can't you?"

"Sure—go!"

The dance floor was packed by then, so I edged around the side of the room until I got to the table where Kita was still standing, chugging a ginger ale like it was Popeye's spinach. Refueling. She smiled when she saw me approach, and I wished so much that she were my girlfriend, that hugging and kissing her could be my normal greeting.

"Hey! I was looking for you," she said.

"I saw you from across the room. What did you say to Danya?"

"I'll tell you if you dance with me."

The band segued into a slow number and Kita put out her arms. *Oh, Lord.* "I don't know how to dance," I said, my voice as quivery as my legs. "Especially, you know, as a boy."

"I think it'll come naturally," she said, placing her left hand on my shoulder and taking my left hand in her right.

"See?" she said. "Easy."

Having Kita's body that close to mine was anything but natural, and yet it felt right. Kids on all sides of us turned to stare, of course, but Kita didn't seem to notice or care. We weren't all snuggled up like a real couple, but our feet seemed to move together to the music, no stumbling or stepping on toes. In fact, dancing with Kita was the closest I was ever likely to come to walking on water.

"So," she said. "You want to know what I told Danya?"

"I do."

"Well, first I told her that I thought she was a horrible bitch, but I think she's proud of that. So then I said that if I ever heard of her even *trying* to hurt you again, or to hurt any of your friends, or any of *my* friends, or anybody at all who couldn't hurt her back, I would personally hunt her down and pull every strand of her ugly yellow hair out by the roots."

My mouth dropped open. "You did? What did she say?"

"Oh, at first she tried to argue that she wasn't the only person who didn't like you. She seems to think she was performing a public service, the idiot."

"She *isn't* the only one, Kita. You know that."

"Maybe, but she's the only one who acted on it."

"So far."

She pulled back to look into my eyes. "Grady, don't say that!"

"I'm just being realistic."

"Well, don't be. Be optimistic."

I was dancing with Kita Charles—if that couldn't make me optimistic, nothing could. "If you say so. After all, you're the one who scared off the big bully for me. My hero. Or heroine."

"I don't know what finally got to her. Apparently, her so-called friends wised up and dumped her, so maybe I was just the last straw. I'm glad to know she actually *has* feelings. That she's not really an escapee from *Night of the Living Dead*."

"Yeah, that would be cause for optimism."

The music kicked into a crazy fast number and, reluctantly, I pulled away from Kita. "I'm no good at this stuff. Anyway, I should get back to the cameras—"

"Grady!" Kita's smile faded a little. "Before you go back, could we talk a minute?"

"Sure." Wasn't that what we'd been doing?

"Out here," she said, pulling me around the corner and into the entrance hall, where the band noise was less deafening. What was this about? I turned around to see if Russ had noticed, but he was talking to Sebastian. What would I say to him? Would he be mad at me? Not that anything had happened to make him mad. Yet.

Kita leaned against the wall, and I stood in front of her, in a perfect position for another kiss.

"Grady," she said, her voice soft and musical. "You know how much I like you, don't you?"

How do you answer a question like that? "I—I hope so," I mumbled. "I like you too, Kita."

"I think you're a wonderful person. Interesting and funny and cute as hell. And you're the nicest . . ." She stopped talking, and her eyes seemed to be pleading with me, but I had no idea what they were asking for. "The thing is, Grady, I made up with Russell. We're back together again."

I think my head may actually have bounced backward from the blow. "Oh," was all I could say.

Kita took my hand in both of hers. "I don't know if it was the right thing to do or not. I feel really confused about all of this. I mean, if Russell weren't in the picture, I would definitely want to be with you, Grady. But Russ is in the picture, and I can't just walk away from him." She sighed. "Especially now, when he's apologized to me so sweetly. He says he wants to try to be a better boyfriend, more respectful of me, and I believe him. I have to at least give him a second chance."

I nodded. "I guess you do," I said, even though my brain was screaming, *No you don't!* My actual feeling was, well, dizziness. In the course of a few minutes I'd found out that Kita had been interested in being my girlfriend, and that the possibility of it actually happening was already over. Apparently, I'd lost the game before I even knew I was playing in it.

"Grady?" Kita said. "Are you okay?"

"Sure," I said, trying to keep my eyes from looking into hers.

She caught them anyway. "I just want you to know that this has nothing to do with what you're going through. I would be crazy about you no matter what gender you were. You believe that, don't you?"

I nodded. I did believe her, but what difference did it make now? She'd chosen Russ.

"I really hope we can still be friends, because I don't want to lose you," she said. When her lips approached mine, I turned my head and they sideswiped my cheek. But that was involuntary; I would still rather have kissed Kita than do anything else on earth. Obviously, my neck muscles had more pride than I did.

I headed back to the cameras, keeping my eyes on my feet, which were no longer walking on water.

Russ looked up as I approached. "Kita tell you the good news?" he asked.

For a second I forgot that Russ didn't know my side of the story. "What?"

"We're back together! Thanks to you, buddy. I owe you one." He held out his hand for me to shake, and I did.

It was impossible not to like Russ, even when he was going out with the girl of your dreams. "Watch it with the macho hand-shaking," I warned as he pumped my arm.

He laughed. "Right. Hey, you mind if I go dance with my girlfriend?"

"Not at all," I said. "I just danced with her myself."

"You beat me!" he said good-humoredly, unaware that in fact he had beaten me. Soundly.

Sebastian was headed in my direction, no doubt to hear what had happened with Kita. I wished I could put off telling him. The whole truth—and nothing but the truth—was lying on my chest like a big rock.

But just then Eve came running toward both of us, sliding in her golden slippers, breathless.

"You will *not* believe what I just saw in the girls' bathroom! Danya is lying on the couch in there, sobbing hysterically. She's cried off all her make-up, and there's green eye shadow smeared on her dress! She's having a complete meltdown!"

"Wow," Sebastian said. "You wanna take a camera in there and get some footage?"

Chapter Twenty-One

I didn't get a lot of sleep that night, which was fine because I had some work to do: tweaking the Christmas Eve script one last time and doing some research online for Charlie's gift. Now that we were friends again, Eve wanted to come too, especially when I told her I was pretty sure it would be our last performance, so I had to add a few lines for her to say. I also had to figure out a few more gifts for people. Something inexpensive, or possibly free, for Eve and Mom and Aunt Gail, because I knew I might have to spend most of my moncy on Charlie this year. I'd already gotten stuff for Sebastian and Laura (they were easy to buy for), and I'd found Dad's gift—the perfect, and perfectly free, gift—two weeks ago. I was doing my gift-giving during the public observance of Christmas this year, not the next day, because this year that was going to be the most important celebration, at least for me.

But having stuff to do didn't keep me from running through my hallway scene with Kita over and over again in my mind. What she'd said. The way she'd looked. The feeling of her hands caressing mine. Was there anything I could have said or done to reverse the final outcome? I reminded myself that Russ had blown his first chance with her; maybe he'd be no better the second time around. Of course, now he had his good friend Grady to come to for advice.

RUSS: Kita says I'm acting like a big macho pig and she's sick of me! What should I do, Grady? Help me!

GRADY: Show that woman who's boss, Russ. Don't let her insult your manhood. Pick her up, throw her over your shoulder, and give her a good smack on the butt. That should bring her around. [twirling his evil mustache] Around to dumping you, that is!

But I didn't feel too bad about what had happened with Kita, or at least I didn't feel *all* bad. If somebody as great as Kita liked me, I figured eventually there would be other girls who would too. And besides, I had four friends now: Sebastian, Eve, Kita, and Russ. I'd never had four friends in my entire life! Four friends was a group, a crowd, a *posse*.

I managed a few hours of sleep and stumbled

downstairs around eight in the morning to find Mom standing over the sink, manhandling a frozen turkey.

"You're up!" we said to each other simultaneously.

"Well, just barely," Mom grumbled. "I still feel terrible, but I forgot to defrost this damn turkey yesterday. It's too big to fit in the microwave—I'm going to have to soak it all day. I'll never get it cooked by five thirty." She picked it up and dropped it into a sink full of warm water, sending a small tsunami across the countertop. "And I haven't even gotten to the store yet to buy the other stuff, the potatoes and green beans and—"

"I have to go out later anyway. Make a list and I'll pick stuff up."

"Oh, honey, would you? I don't know how much of this celebration I'm going to be able to manage today."

"Mom, leave the turkey in the sink. I'll get Laura and Charlie to help me make dinner. Dad, too."

She gave me a terrified look.

"Well, okay, not Dad. But the rest of us should be able to do it. How much work can it be to make some mashed potatoes and green beans?"

"And the pudding. Don't forget the pudding."

But she was heading for the stairs already, gladly handing it over to me.

"And pudding. I won't forget." I had no idea how you made pudding, or even green beans, for that matter—Mom had always done all the cooking, and I'd paid no attention—but there must be a book somewhere in the kitchen that would tell me.

"Just call me if you need anything," Mom said, her voice disappearing back into the bedroom.

An hour later, just as I was about to nod off into a pile of cookbooks, Laura appeared, in an extremely sunny mood. Jason must have lived up to expectations.

"Mom gave me a list of stuff for you to buy for dinner," she said, dropping the list on the table. "She said *we're* doing the cooking. That'll be fun!"

I yawned and forced myself to wake up. "I found out how you roast a turkey. And mashed potatoes and green beans are easy enough. But I don't know how to do the pudding. How do you make pudding?"

Laura made that face with which she silently calls me a moron. "You open a couple of those little square boxes, add milk, and stir."

"It comes in boxes?"

"God, Grady, have you ever been in a kitchen

before? This is a refrigerator. That's a stove."

"Okay, okay. As long as you know how to do it." I grabbed the list. "I'll get this stuff. You keep working on defrosting the turkey. You have to change the water to keep it warm."

She poked the lump in the sink. "It's hard as a rock!"

"I know. The recipe says a turkey this size has to cook for four hours. Which means it should go into the oven around one o'clock."

"What if it isn't thawed out?"

I shrugged. "I guess we'll have to put it in anyway. Won't it thaw out in the oven?"

"How should I know? I've never cooked a turkey."

"Well, I don't know what else to do," I said. "I'm going to be gone for a couple of hours, so—"

"A couple of hours? Where are you going?"

"Before I go to the store, I have one more present to buy, and I have to go to Connecticut to get it." I was so excited about my find that I sort of wanted to tell Laura about it, but I was afraid she couldn't be trusted not to blab it to everybody else before I got back.

"Connecticut? They don't sell this thing in Massachusetts? Are you crazy?"

"Probably."

"Do Mom and Dad know you're doing this?"

"No. When Dad comes down, just tell him I had some last-minute errands to do, okay? Could you please try to keep this small secret?"

"Tell me what you're getting in Connecticut."

"Can't. It's a surprise."

"For me?" That idea got her a little excited.

"Well, not exactly, but in a way. In a way, it's for all of us."

She frowned and turned back to the turkey. "Secrets are stupid."

"So," I said, "did you have fun at the dance?"

Her features unclouded, and a look of serenity settled over her face. "All I can say is: Oh. My. God."

"Hold that thought," I said, then grabbed the car keys and made my escape before another family member woke up.

It took longer to find the place in Connecticut than I thought it would, and longer to negotiate with the people in charge. At first my story didn't satisfy them, but I pled my case until we finally came to an agreement, and, after settling my gift into the backseat, I was on my way.

By the time I did the grocery shopping and got back, pulling the car into the garage and closing the door behind me as quickly as possible, it was almost one o'clock. I could hear the pandemonium before I opened the door.

"Finally!" Laura shrieked when I walked in. She and Charlie and the entire kitchen floor were all soaking wet from using the faucet sprayer on the turkey, and obviously on each other, too. "Where have you been? I preheated the oven, like the recipe said to, but this stupid turkey is still frozen!"

Dad came in from the dining room. "Oh, there you are, Grady. How does your mother set the table? Does the fork go on the left or the right?"

"Left, I think," I said, squinting my eyes and trying to visualize it. On a normal evening we were lucky if somebody managed to get the silverware matched up to a plate, much less on the correct side of it. "Is Mom still in bed?"

He nodded. "I think we should let her sleep until the last minute so she can enjoy the evening. I'm sure she'll be feeling better by five o'clock."

Always the optimist. Kita would like Dad.

"Would somebody please tell me what to do with this turkey?" Laura yelled.

"Let's throw it out and buy a different one," Charlie said.

"Now, now," Dad said. "I'm sure it'll be fine.

Why don't you just dry it off and stick it in the oven? Just turn the oven up a little higher than it says to in the book—that'll probably do it."

I wasn't sure he was right about that, but what choice did we have? And then I saw Dad head for the garage door.

"Where are you going?" I cried, jumping in front of him.

He backed up, surprised. "Well, since I'm not doing too well in the dining room, I thought I'd bring in the wood for the fireplaces for tonight."

"I'll do that!" I said. "Don't go out there, okay?"

"Why not?"

"Grady, you have to help me with this turkey," Laura said. "Charlie already dropped it once."

"That wasn't *my* fault," Charlie said. "You threw it at me!"

I stood in front of the door, my arms out at my sides. "Okay!" I said. "I'll tell you all this much. There is something in the garage that I don't want anyone to see until the performance tonight. It's a surprise. If you go out there now, the whole thing will be ruined!"

Laura rolled her eyes. "And you say *I'm* overdramatic."

"What is it?" Charlie asked.

Laura glared at him. "You dumbo, didn't you hear him? If it's a surprise, why would he tell *you* what it is? Besides, it's just something weird he had to go to Connecticut to get."

Thank you, Laura.

Charlie wrinkled his nose. "Connecticut? What do they have in Connecticut that we don't have in Massachusetts?"

"All right," Dad said, shushing them both. "I think we can all manage to wait a few hours to see what Grady's surprise is. There's plenty for us to do in here. You can bring in the wood, Grady—there's a pile outside the back garage door."

"After he helps me get the turkey in the oven!" Laura demanded.

"After you help Laura get the turkey in the oven," Dad agreed. "And I'll go back to setting the table. Does anybody know where we keep the napkins? Or the candlesticks? Or the dishes?"

Chapter Twenty-Two

Laura and Eve were in their dresses before five o'clock. Dad, of course, had been wearing his outfit for hours. Sebastian fit surprisingly well into Charlie's old Tiny Tim outfit and was enjoying using his cane as a sword with which to attack a pile of dirty socks cowering in the corner of my bedroom.

Charlie and I were doing less well. Since Mom hadn't been able to tailor any of Dad's old outfits for us, we were trying to find anything we could in the costume box that came close to fitting. All the pants were far too long for Charlie, so he just left on his jeans—and, what the heck, his sneakers too—and wore a big gray shirt over the top that made him look more like a nineteenth-century prison inmate than Bob Cratchit's kid. I could wear Dad's pants, although they had to be belted at the waist and rolled at the ankles. With a tucked-in shirt, suspenders, and a too-large vest, I looked like a circus clown who'd lost his wig.

But the biggest problem was Mom. She wouldn't get up. Laura had gone in several times to offer to help her get dressed, but had been met by a sleepy refusal. Finally, Dad had been sent to rouse her. He came out smiling. "She'll be up any minute. Nothing to worry about." Still, the rest of us worried.

Laura put in a call to Aunt Gail. "When are you coming over? Mom won't get up!"

Apparently, Aunt Gail's answer was something like, "We're running late too. Michael was all dressed in that cute little outfit your mother made him, and then he pooped all over himself."

"Eww." Laura made a face.

"If we're late, we'll just pretend to be . . . guests who are late!" Gail said.

"But what about Mom?" Laura asked.

"Make some coffee. Hold it under her nose."

Not bad advice, we decided. Eve actually knew how to brew coffee too, so we wouldn't accidentally make our sick mother sicker.

As Laura went upstairs with the coffee mug, Sebastian peeped out the curtained front window. "Grady! There are a million people out there!"

"Nah," Charlie said. "Usually about a hundred, hundred and twenty. I bet nobody's standing near those melting bears, are they?"

"As far away as possible," Sebastian said.

I opened the oven, which I hadn't dared to peek in for hours. The turkey didn't look bad. Well, maybe a little bit burned on the very top, possibly because we'd turned the oven up to five hundred degrees. But basically it looked like a regular turkey, ready to carve. Amazing. I got the pot holders, and Sebastian helped me take it out and put it on top of the stove.

"There's a fancy turkey platter someplace," I said.

"I know where it is," Eve said, heading for the dining-room pantry.

The three of us managed, with pot holders, forks, and when necessary our hands, to transfer the turkey from the pan to the platter. Mom would have made gravy, but we were under no illusions that we could do that.

The potatoes were mashed, the beans were cooked, the rolls were baked, and they were all waiting to be nuked at the last minute. The pudding was milked and stirred and refrigerated. We had actually made a meal that appeared to be edible.

"She's sitting up and drinking the coffee!" Laura announced as she came running back downstairs.

"See, I told you," Dad said. He'd just laid the fires in both rooms and was dusting off his pants. He checked his watch. "Almost time. Grady, where are our scripts?"

"Upstairs—I'll get them," I said.

"We should have had them sooner," Laura complained. "So we could learn our lines."

"Don't worry about the script," I said. "I want it to be a surprise."

"God, you're like *Mr.* Surprise these days," she said.

Had to give her that one. The past month had been one shock after the other, but I was beginning to like not knowing what would happen next. Now that I knew there were people who'd help me roll with the punches, it was kind of exciting.

As I came out of my room with the scripts, Mom opened her bedroom door and shuffled out in her house slippers. She was still in her nightgown, her old, crummy robe thrown over it, the collar half tucked in, the hem ripped out in the back. Her hair was a mess, and her eyes were puffy slits. She sipped from the coffee cup.

"I'm up," she said. "I feel better, but I'm not putting on that dumb dress. It's too tight in the waist. And besides . . . I don't want to."

I laughed and handed her a script. "Mom, I think you're dressed perfectly for my version of the play."

"Why? Is it set in a hospital?" Her slippers made a shooshing sound on the steps.

Although I could tell that Dad was a little taken aback by Mom's appearance, nobody said anything about her showing up in ancient flannel sleepwear. Fortunately, she caught sight of herself in the hall mirror.

"Oh, for God's sake, I can't go out there looking like this!"

We stared at her helplessly for a minute, and then Charlie had an idea. "Take off the robe and put on that big black overcoat of Dad's!"

Dad approved the change—what choice did he have at this point? The show must go on and all that. Laura found a bonnet and helped Mom tuck her straggly hair under it so she bore at least some vague resemblance to the rest of us.

I handed out the rest of the scripts at the last possible moment so nobody would read ahead. Dad and Sebastian put on their frock coats, hats, and mufflers, and Sebastian stood on a chair while I helped hoist him onto Dad's shoulders. We were always glad the Victorians wore so many layers of clothing, because Dad liked having the windows open so he could hear the spectators' comments. At five thirty I turned on the microphones and slowly pulled back the curtains, as I'd done for ten years. Ten years is an awfully long run for any play.

The audience applauded, although as we paraded through the dining room and into the living room, there were some audible remarks about the new costumes on display. "What's she got on?" and "That's not what they usually wear" and "Who's that?"

As always, Dad and Tiny Tim entered last, Dad heartily shouting out, "We're home, Mrs. Cratchit. We're home!" Unfortunately, Sebastian was holding his script in front of his face and didn't duck soon enough when they came through the living room doorway. His cap absorbed most of the blow, but it made Dad stagger, and we could hear our audience laugh. Good. The fun was just beginning.

Dad swung Sebastian down from his shoulders and improvised a line: "Are you fine as feathers, my good son?" *Fine as feathers?*

"Fine as ever I have been, Father," Sebastian answered, smiling and leaning on his cane. These two, I thought, belonged on Broadway.

In Dad's original version, Mom came flying up to him when he entered, gave him a kiss, then took the coats, hats, and mufflers from Dad and Tiny Tim and hung them up. Fortunately, my new script didn't call for her to do any flying—the poor woman could barely walk. She read her lines in a tired voice from a chair by the Christmas tree while Dad and Sebastian took off their own outerwear.

MRS. CRATCHIT: Mind you, Mr. Cratchit, are the reindeer on the roof again? And the singers at the front door? And the dollies still goin' in circles? And the bears a-smellin' up the neighborhood?

MR. CRATCHIT: Yes, my dear. Things are just as they should be.

Dad read his part in a booming voice, although he looked a little confused by the new lines. I stepped forward for my line as Mrs. Cratchit lapsed into a fit of coughing.

GRADY: And yet, things do change, Father. You need only look at me to see the truth of that!

EVE: Yes, this year has seen your Angela become your Grady and exchange her long dresses for his sturdy trousers.

LAURA: And trade her long locks for the haircut of a boy.

GRADY: Things as they should be, Father, are not things unchanging.
[to the audience] We shall see many changes as this magical evening does progress.

I wondered if the audience outside was as stunned as the one inside. I couldn't hear much noise from the front lawn anymore, and the actors themselves were trying to surreptitiously read ahead to see what other surprises lay in store for them. Sebastian hobbled forward on his crutch.

TINY TIM: As the sick may become well, so may the unsure become confident.

Sebastian had written that line himself and was quite proud of it. Charlie stepped up next.

CHARLIE: Perhaps before this enchanted night is through, you too will dance to a tune, Tim!
TINY TIM: 'Twould be a timely tune that tickled the timid Tim to tap his toes!

Fortunately, Sebastian had had the script all week, so he'd had time to practice this, his favorite line, which he delivered with relish. The audience really laughed this time. They got it now: This was not the quiet, somber fare of years past. Dad smiled nervously, then bent to light the fire, as he always did at this point in the performance, and the rest of us crowded around the tree, waiting for gifts. I could tell Laura was looking for the directions which would tell her who to hand which gift to, but they weren't in her script. I stood again when the fire was lit.

GRADY: Good people, this year the gifts you open are from me. These days past I have been given by you many gifts: foremost of all, the gift of understanding. And so I return what offerings I can to you.

Dad nodded as I handed small packages to Laura and Eve. The only direction in the script for most of the gift-opening part of the show was "Respond however you would like." Only Dad's part had scripted dialogue. I knew that that probably made the girls nervous; they hadn't done any improvising before.

Eve pulled from her box an article I'd clipped from the newspaper. The headline, which she read out loud, was POLICE TO LEAD SELF-DEFENSE COURSE.

EVE: [holding it up for all to see] Why, whatever is this, Grady?

GRADY: I thought it would be a good activity for the two of us to engage in together, my dear friend. It has no cost, and yet the benefits for meek ones such as you and me will, I think, be great. Would you do me the honor of accompanying me? I have already set our names down on the scroll at the police station.

EVE: Oh, this notion fills me with . . . glee. Thank you ever so much.

I nodded to her and waited for Laura's reaction. Laura took a small silver square from her box and pulled it open. Eye makeup in twelve shades with two tiny brushes.

LAURA: [confused] I have never seen such a thing, dear brother.

GRADY: Oh, surely you have, Laura. It's eye shadow. Your favorite kind.

LAURA: But, I did think . . .

She glanced out the window, clearly at a loss for words. I helped her out.

GRADY: . . . that eye shadow was not invented in the nineteenth century? Women have always found ways to decorate themselves, dear sister. The pursuit of beauty was not invented yesterday. And though it is of little interest to me, I know that it is quite important to you.

And besides, there's no use trying to change people until they're ready to change. You pretty much have to do that particular hard work by yourself. Laura whispered a thank-you and sat daintily back on her heels.

Sebastian's box was larger than the others. He was surprised by it, I could tell, and he began to improvise.

TINY TIM: You know, dear brother, there is not a worldly thing I need when I have my whole family around me like this. That is the best Christmas present.

Boy, was he laying it on thick—Dad must be ready to adopt him. He kept ripping at the paper, though, and eventually got down to my carefully chosen gift: a T-shirt with a picture of Napoleon Dynamite on it and the words I'VE GOT YOUR BACK.

TINY TIM: Awesome! [then, remembering who he was and where] Thank you, dear brother, for such a warm article of clothing, which also proclaims my devotion to a true champion!

GRADY: As Father always taught us, one good geek deserves another.

That got a nice laugh too. Next I handed small boxes to Mom and Dad. Charlie looked pissed off at having to wait for his. Mom smiled weakly and opened the lid on hers.

MRS. CRATCHIT: Why, 'tis a scroll of paper. A proclamation, perhaps. [reading it] "I, your son Grady, promise to help you cook dinner two nights a week, thereby saving several nights for other persons in my family who might also want to learn the non-gender-specific ritual of preparing the evening meal." Goodness, this is a gift I am most grateful for, my dearest . . . son.

Mom gave me a wink, and I knew she really was happy. It was an obvious gift, but one I hadn't come up with until that morning as I was paging through the cookbooks. It cost me nothing but time, and in fact I did want to learn more about cooking. Maybe someday I'd learn how to make pudding that didn't come in a box.

MRS. CRATCHIT: Our son has given thoughtful gifts. I await impatiently the opening of Mr. Cratchit's box. [another bout of coughing]

Dad opened his box and lifted out the flyer I'd taken from the bulletin board at Atkins Pharmacy the last time I was there. He unfolded it carefully, held it near a candle, and began to read it.

MR. CRATCHIT: "Buxton Little Theater needs help! We are particularly in need of volunteers who can build sets for our productions. We're also looking for more talented actors to help us with our spring show, *Oliver!* If you can use a saw, carry a tune, or project to the balcony, please come to our auditions on January fourteenth." Well now, does my son think this description fits his father?

GRADY: I do indeed, Father. Both the sawing and the projecting.

MR. CRATCHIT: Not the singing?

MRS. CRATCHIT: Children, your father sang quite a lovely baritone in days of old.

GRADY: Well then, he's a perfect fit! And of course, we know that the original *Oliver, Oliver Twist*, was written by our favorite storyteller, Mr. Charles Dickens himself.

MR. CRATCHIT: [back on script now] It does sound like a vocation I would enjoy. And yet, it could take time away from my family obligations.

MRS. CRATCHIT: [thoughtfully] Yes. Father might have to give up doing some of his productions around the house. What would you children think of that?

GRADY: I think Rudolph would miss us more than we'd miss him.

LAURA: I'd rather see a performance than be in one.

CHARLIE: It's time to retire the old bears anyway.

TINY TIM: Father! Could I go to the auditions with you?

Okay, that line wasn't in the script. Clearly, Sebastian felt comfortable throwing in whatever he wanted. I was glad he did, though. I think it got my father over the hump of realizing what we meant. He swallowed, then spoke, his voice a bit thick.

MR. CRATCHIT: Of course, Tim. We'll sally forth together. Things do change, as your brother has rightly said, and I'm glad to find this new challenge. Thank you, Grady.

MRS. CRATCHIT: Yes, we all thank you, son.

Meanwhile, Charlie was getting really tired of waiting.

CHARLIE: I say, Grady, haven't you forgotten someone?

GRADY: No, I don't think I have, Charlie.

CHARLIE: I don't even see another box under the tree for me!

GRADY: [standing] Of course not. Your gift couldn't fit under the Christmas tree, dear brother. Let me get it from its hiding place.

I was so excited. I'd been waiting for this moment all day. Nobody but me had gone out to the garage, and, as they'd assured me at the shelter, Betsy was not a barker, so the surprise would be complete. I clipped on her leash and let her out the back door to pee before her introduction to the family. She was so happy to see me again, she leaped up and stuck her tongue right in my mouth. In case you were wondering, French kisses from a dog are not really that desirable.

Betsy had been angelic in the car on the drive home, but I guess being locked in the garage alone all afternoon had driven up her energy level. As soon as we walked through the kitchen door, she began to pull on the leash, her nails skittering across the floor. She yanked me through the dining room and into the living room, as the outdoor audience howled and laughed, and the indoor actors screamed, all of us completely breaking character.

CHARLIE: It's a dog! I got a dog!

GRADY: This is Betsy—she's a—sit down, girl. Sit down. Betsy, sit!

CHARLIE: [grabbing Betsy around the neck] Grady got me a dog!

MRS. CRATCHIT: Grady, are you out of your mind?

MR. CRATCHIT: You know your mother is . . . oh, what a friendly puppy!

TINY TIM: I didn't think you'd really be able to find one—

GRADY: There's an Internet site where all the shelters post what dogs they have. You just plug in your zip code and you find out where the nearest one is.

LAURA: This is why you drove to Connecticut? To get this mutt?

MRS. CRATCHIT: [cringing in her chair by the fireplace] What were you thinking, Grady? I'm allergic to dogs! Get her off the couch!

CHARLIE: [clinging to Betsy's neck] She's my dog!

GRADY: Listen to me a minute. Betsy is a standard poodle. Aunt Gail was telling me the other day that some dogs don't shed, so I went online and found out that poodles don't shed, and that some people who are allergic to other dogs aren't allergic to poodles. I explained the situation at the shelter, and they said we can bring her back if Mom has a bad reaction. But I thought we could at least try it. Charlie wants a dog so badly, and he needs a buddy to hang out with, too.

CHARLIE: I do, Mom, I do!

EVE: This is a poodle? It doesn't look like one.

GRADY: She isn't shaved. You don't have to shave them with those silly puffs of fur around their tails and ankles. This is how they look naturally.

There was actually a moment of near silence as Charlie and Betsy climbed all over each other and the rest of us watched. Then, suddenly, we remembered that we had an audience. One by one, we turned to look at them. They were staring right back at us, as if we were the newest reality TV show. Dad tried to get us back on track.

MR. CRATCHIT: Well, Mrs. Cratchit, I suppose we shall see what we shall see. The animal will spend the night in young Charles's room. And now I'm sure dinner is ready and waiting for us. We mustn't let it get cold.

MRS. CRATCHIT: [still staring at Betsy] I suppose so. I have no idea.

GRADY: Yes, Father and Mother, please take a seat at the dinner table. Your children will serve you your Christmas feast tonight!

With a backward glance at Betsy, Mom heaved herself out of the chair and headed for the dining room. As she passed me, she hissed, "We'll discuss this later."

Dad pulled out the chair for her, and she flopped into it. Laura, Eve, and I brought the food in from the kitchen. Tiny Sebastian limped to his chair, and I signaled Charlie to keep a tight hold on the dog, which was clearly his preference anyway. We gathered at the table, a somewhat more disheveled group than usual, and Dad began his blessing, which I had rewritten for him only slightly.

> MR. CRATCHIT: To have my family gathered together on Christmas Eve, to have them all together at the close of another year—there is nothing in life that makes me happier. It is a joy that no Scrooge will ever understand.

He stopped here to decide if he really had to say the next line. Then, looking out the window, he did.

> MR. CRATCHIT: It has been delightful to include all of you in our festivities these many years, but this evening we must bid you a fond farewell, at least as actors in a play.

There was a groan from outside the window, but it was eclipsed by the slamming of the kitchen door.

> AUNT GAIL: What an ungrateful wench am I to be so late for the holiday gathering! I hope I have not missed the turkey!

She sped into the dining room in her Victorian outfit, Michael on her shoulder dressed in a gold-and-white striped onesie that made him look like a huge bumblebee.

The arrival of a new and exciting guest was too much for Betsy. She escaped Charlie's grasp and scooted under the table, which made Mrs. Cratchit scream and Tiny Tim drop his crutch. Before Mr. Cratchit could stop her, Betsy had jumped up on Aunt Gail's apron and was trying to pull her bonnet off by the strings. Michael, terrified, began to wail.

AUNT GAIL: Good God, there's a dog in here!

CHARLIE: She's my dog!

AUNT GAIL: Get down!

MR. CRATCHIT: [yanking at Betsy's collar] We were just giving the blessing, dear sister. Please have a seat and we'll enjoy our feast!

Gail managed to get away from Betsy and proceed down the table to the empty chair, giving Mrs. Cratchit a look of bewilderment.

MR. CRATCHIT: [letting go of Betsy's collar to raise his glass] Let us drink a toast to all our Christmases past, and all the wonderful ones yet to come. 'Tis a season like no other!

With all our hands in the air, Betsy saw her chance. Her big front paws flopping on the table, she reached her snout across and grabbed the turkey in her mouth. It occurred to me then that I probably should have fed her while she was waiting out in the garage.

Mr. Cratchit and Charlie both chased Betsy around the table and then into the living room, where she ran under the Christmas tree, got a strand of lights caught over her head, and almost brought down the entire spruce. Fortunately, Mr. Cratchit broke the tree's fall, and only a few ornaments were demolished. By the time Charlie caught Betsy, our audience was in hysterics, and he stopped and gave a low bow to his fans.

MRS. CRATCHIT: [her coat flapping open] Close those damn curtains, Grady! For God's sake, close those damn curtains!

GRADY: Wait! There's one thing we musn't forget on Christmas Eve.

I gestured wildly to Sebastian, and he climbed onto his chair, waving his cane to the crowd as though he were on a parade float.

TINY TIM: God bless us, every one!

I ran to the curtains and closed them as quickly as possible. Dad switched off the indoor microphones, and we waited in silence for the howls of our neighbors to subside into mere laughter.

Chapter Twenty-Three

As it turned out, even Betsy couldn't eat that turkey. The outside was burned, but the inside was cold and pink. Mom made Dad put it in a trash bag and take it right out to the garbage can before anybody got food poisoning from it. Dad made a quick run to a convenience store, too, to pick up some dog food before everyone closed for the holiday. Hey, I'd never had a pet before—you couldn't expect me to have thought of everything. At least I'd gotten a collar and a leash.

We sat around the table eating mashed potatoes, green beans, rolls, and chocolate pudding while we listened to the neighbors come to their senses and leave. People stood around in groups talking to each other for a ridiculously long time. Even though I'd closed the windows, we could still hear a few shouted-out comments.

"Best one ever!" a male voice declared.

"Do it again next year. Please?" asked a child.

"Thank you for years of enjoyment!" a woman

yelled. "You've got more nerve than I do!"

Finally, they were all gone, and we dared to begin to speak to each other.

"Well, I guess that was the last one," Dad said sadly.

"And no one will ever forget it," Mom said, shaking her head.

"You went out with a bang!" Sebastian said.

Dad smiled at him. "You and me are gonna knock 'em dead at those auditions, kiddo!"

Sebastian squirmed with pleasure.

"Now, about the dog," Mom began.

"Mom, she's been in the house for an hour already and you aren't sneezing or anything!" Charlie said. "She's the perfect dog! Please, can I keep her?"

Betsy was at least pretending to be the perfect dog, now that all the excitement was over and she'd had some dinner. She lay at Charlie's feet, turning over on her back to let him scratch her stomach.

"Charlie, it's too soon to know if I'm having a reaction to the dog. We'll have to wait and see. But if we do keep her . . ."

By which we all knew the chances were very good that we would. Mom laid down a few rules about who was going to do the feeding and the walking (Charlie), and where Betsy was going to sleep (Charlie's room), and where Betsy was *not* going to sleep (the couch), but when Betsy put her big snout on Mom's lap and looked up into her eyes, we all heard the sigh of resignation. That dog wasn't going anywhere.

By the next morning Mom was feeling almost normal—the flu was gone and no allergic symptoms had appeared. We opened our "real" presents, but personally I didn't think any of them were better than the ones I'd come up with the night before. Sebastian would be very glad to hear I'd gotten a cell phone, though.

One of the first calls I intended to make on it was to the GLBT group Ms. Unger had given me the number for. I wanted to find out when they held their meetings. Even though things seemed pretty good right now, I knew there would be plenty of stuff to deal with down the road. Like, how far would my transition go? Did I want to take hormones? Would I eventually have surgery to make my body fit my soul? When I met new people, should I tell them the truth right away? What about girls I was interested in? It wouldn't be easy—I knew that. I'd need more help than my family and friends could give me to figure it all out, but at least now I knew they were on my side. And that was a huge gift.

Mom fulfilled another of Charlie's wishes by announcing that she intended to look for a teaching job for the fall term next year and so did Susan. They were going to send the boys to public school. She said she was tired of being home all day and a little bit jealous of Gail's ability to have a life outside of motherhood. Gail got up and gave her a hug for admitting that, and didn't even rush to wash her hands afterward. I don't think Charlie actually heard the reason he was going to public school—he was making too much noise doing the happy dance with Betsy.

By the time we all sat down to dinner—an edible one this time, which Aunt Gail had come early to help prepare—the events of the night before had already solidified into legend. Mom in her nightgown, Michael in his bumblebee outfit, Sebastian banging his head, Betsy grabbing the turkey and knocking over the tree: All of it had, in only twenty-four hours, become hilarious. We repeated the lines that had gotten the biggest laughs and became hysterical ourselves. It was the best Christmas ever.

Sometimes it's hard to remember that by tomorrow or next week or at least next year, the stuff that seems so awful today might actually be funny. That what makes you miserable today will later on in life be a good story to tell your friends.

Why does that happen? I don't know. Things change. People change. We spend a long time trying to figure out how to act like ourselves, and then, if we're lucky, we finally figure out that being ourselves has nothing to do with acting. If you don't believe it, just look at me, the kid in the middle of the football field, smiling.

References

The following books were of great help to me in the researching of this book.

Bornstein, Kate. *Gender Outlaw: On Men, Women and the Rest of Us*. New York: Vintage Books, 1995.

Bornstein, Kate. *My Gender Workbook*. New York: Routledge, 1998.

Boylan, Jennifer Finney. *She's Not There: A Life in Two Genders*. New York: Broadway Books, 2003.

Brown, Mildred L., and Chloe Ann Rounsley. *True Selves: Understanding Transsexualism*. San Francisco: Jossey-Bass, 1996.

Feinberg, Leslie. *Transgender Warriors: Making History from Joan of Arc to Dennis Rodman*. Boston: Beacon Press, 1997.

O'Keefe, Tracie, and Katrina Fox, eds. *Finding the Real Me, True Tales of Sex and Gender Diversity*. San Francisco: Jossey-Bass, 2003.

Other Books of Interest

Beyond Magenta: Transgender Teens Speak Out, by Susan Kuklin, Candlewick Press, 2014

Helping Your Transgender Teen: A Guide for Parents by Irwin Krieger, Genderwise Press, 2011

Redefining Realness: My Path to Womanhood, Identity, Love & So Much More, by Janet Mock, Atria Books, 2014

Rethinking Normal by Katie Rain Hill, Simon & Schuster, 2014

Some Assembly Required by Arin Andrews, Simon & Schuster, 2014

The Transgender Child: A Handbook for Families and Professionals, by Stephanie Brill and Rachel Pepper, Cleis Press, 2008

The Transgender Guidebook: Keys to a Successful Transition, by Anne L. Boedecker, PhD, CreateSpace Independent Publishing Platform, 2011

Transgender 101: A Simple Guide to a Complex Issue, by Nicholas M. Teich, Columbia University Press, 2012

Transgender History by Susan Stryker, Seal Press, 2008

Transparent: Love, Family, and Living the T with Transgender Teenagers, by Cris Beam, Harcourt, Inc., 2007

Resources

Advocates for Youth
www.advocatesforyouth.org

This group advocates for changes to improve delivery of adolescent sexual health information and services. One topic addressed on the website is the health and rights of transgender youth.

Camp Aranu'tiq
www.camparanutiq.org

An overnight camp for transgender and gender-variant children and teens

Gay, Lesbian & Straight Education Network (GLSEN)
www.glsen.org

The mission of GLSEN is to insure that each member of every school community is valued and respected regardless of sexual orientation or gender identity or expression. The organization works to educate teachers, students, and the public at large about the damaging effects of homophobia and heterosexism in schools.

Gay-Straight Alliance Network
www.gsanetwork.org

Empowers youth activists to fight homophobia and transphobia in schools.

Gender Spectrum
www.genderspectrum.org

Provides an array of services to help families, schools, and organizations understand and address gender identity and gender expression.

GLAAD Transgender Resources
www.glaad.org/transgender/resources

List of trans organizations and programs put together by GLAAD (Gay and Lesbian Alliance Against Defamation).

Intersex Society of North America (ISNA)
www.isna.org

A resource for people seeking information and advice about atypical reproductive anatomies.

It Gets Better
www.itgetsbetter.org

Video project that spreads the message of hope for LGBTQ teens.

National Center for Transgender Equality (NCTE)
www.transequality.org

Monitors federal activity and communicates this activity to its members around the country, providing congressional education and establishing a center of expertise on issues of importance to transgender people.

Parents, Families and Friends of Lesbians and Gays (PFLAG)
www.pflag.org

Promotes the health and well-being of lesbian, gay, bisexual, and transgender persons and their families by offering support, education and advocacy.

The Trevor Project
www.thetrevorproject.org
866-488-7386

Provides crisis intervention and suicide prevention for GLBTQ youth.

Trans Youth Family Allies (TYFA)
www.imatyfa.org

Partners with educators, service providers, and communities to develop supportive environments in which gender may be expressed and respected.

TransActive Gender Center
www.transactiveonline.org

Provides a range of services and expertise to empower transgender and gender-diverse youth and their families.

TransGenderCare
www.transgendercare.com

Educational website which contains a large archive of health information, both medical and psychological, for transgender people and their family and friends.

Transgender Legal Defense & Education Fund
www.transgenderlegal.org

Committed to ending discrimination based on gender identity and expression, and to achieving equality for transgender people.

True Colors Fund
http://truecolorsfund.org

Works to end homelessness among LGBT youth.

The World Professional Association for Transgender Health
www.wpath.org

Educational organization devoted to transgender health.

Youth Guardian Services
www.youth-guard.org

A youth-run organization that provides support services on the Internet to gay, lesbian, bisexual, transgender, questioning, and supportive straight youth.

love, lust, laughs, loss, life.

"Sones captures the ache of first love. Readers may find themselves laughing, crying, and wanting to believe the unreliable, well-developed narrator."
—*SLJ*

★ "A sharp, honest story about overcoming grief. . . . Raw, and very funny."—*Booklist*, starred review

"Romantic and sexy . . . will leave teenage readers sighing with recognition and satisfaction."—*Kirkus Reviews*

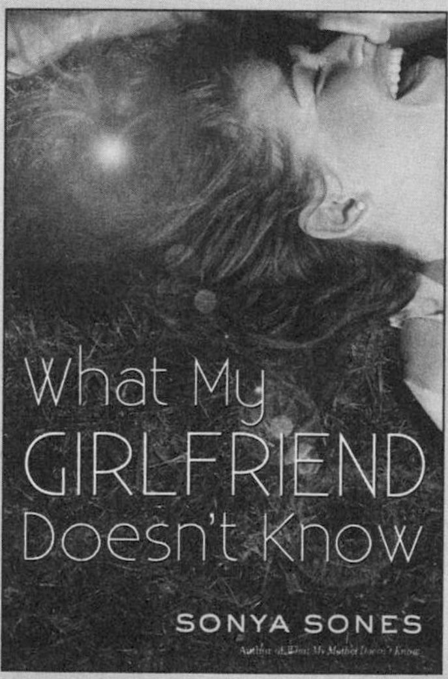

★ "The story of a thrilling and faltering first love."—*Booklist*, starred review

PRINT AND EBOOK EDITIONS AVAILABLE • From SIMON & SCHUSTER BFYR • simonandschuster.com/teen